Reinaldo the Magnificent

Written by Sukoshi Rice

Illustrated by C.S. Rogers

Sukoshi Rice

Ageless Hipster Press

PO Box 1602

Murphy, NC 28906 USA

ISBN-13: 978-1-970038-03-3

THIS BOOK IS DEDICATED
TO CHILDREN EVERYWHERE,
ESPECIALLY TO RASTA AND PABLO,
WHO HEARD THESE STORIES FIRST.
AND THANK YOU TO JULES, MY FIRST READER.

Sukoshi Rice

TABLE OF CONTENTS

Sukoshi Rice

Reinaldo the Magnificent!

"Hey, Reinaldo, come down here and help with dinner!" The words blasted up the stairs into Reinaldo's room where he was busy teaching his little dog Waffles the disappearing trick. With Waffles by his side, Reinaldo twirled his shiny black magician's cape, waving his magic wand in the air.

"Come help me NOW!" His mom sounded *so* grouchy! Reinaldo remembered a time she had been so sweet. She used to have cookies waiting when he and Tiffany got home from school. She used to have dinner all made so she could kiss their father when he came through the door from work.

Now that she had a job too, she was always tired, rushed, and cranky.

Reinaldo carefully lay his magic wand down on his night table and took off his cape. Wearing his cape into the kitchen, or trying to wear it at the dinner table would definitely mean another trip to his room. As hard as he wished his parents believed in magic, or even remembered how to play, they seemed to wish just as hard that he would just grow up and hurry up about it. But helping with dinner wasn't bad. It could even be fun, especially with Waffles by his side.

"C'mon Waffles, we've gotta help Mom," Reinaldo called, bouncing out the door and down the stairs. Waffles ran beside him, excited and ready to help by catching any food that might fall.

Penny, his mom, was running around trying to get dinner made and do ten things at once. The zipper on her skirt was jammed and she was desperate to get out of that skirt and put on her jeans, but she was stuck! This put her in a bad mood to start dinner and she wished the whole family would just take care of themselves and let her relax and read the paper after work, too! Tiffany, his teenaged sister, was flipping through a magazine looking at haircuts. She was supposed to be making a salad or something, but she was stuck at the page of big poufy hairstyles. Every once in a while, Penny would give a big sigh and say, "Tiffany, please," and Tiffany would look up and do something for a second. At least she wasn't on her phone! Then Penny would have had a *total* meltdown!

Oh man, Reinaldo thought, watching his mom freaking out around the kitchen, I wish she believed in magic! She'd have so much more *fun* and she'd *be* more fun, too! Maybe he could wave his magic wand and dinner would just appear....? But no way was he going to suggest *that*, especially with her already so touchy! It was easier just to peel the carrots by hand.

In the living room, sprawled on a big fat Lazy Boy was a big fat lazy boy named Dan, Reinaldo's dad. Reinaldo had heard stories about all the fun his mom used to have with his dad and what a great guy he was. Gee, that's hard to imagine, Reinaldo thought, looking at Dan, sprawled in his chair. He used to be so fit and healthy-looking. Now he was all soft and tired, with his belly getting paunchy and big. Worst of it was he used to have energy to play. "Go out for a pass!" he'd yell while Reinaldo scrambled after a little kiddie football spinning low across the lawn. Now he was tired all the time, and hardly ever wanted to play ball or do anything but watch sports on TV and take naps.

Yuck, what a weird family! Reinaldo thought, bending down to give Waffles a hug. They're either lying around or so crazed they can't slow down! He turned away from the refrigerator, a bag of carrots in his hand, and bumped straight into Tiffany.

"Hey, watch out!" she squawked at him.

But he didn't care. Tiffany wasn't a problem. She was too interested in herself to cause him any bother. All he had to do to get her off his back was walk by a mirror. She'd instantly get lost looking at her own reflection.

When the whole family was finally around the table eating, Penny turned to Reinaldo. "Sweetheart, since your birthday is coming up a week from Saturday, I thought we could have a little party for you here. Would you like that?"

Reinaldo nodded, his dark eyes dancing. He thought about the kind of party he would like to have, the people he would invite, and then his mind switched gears. "Hey," he said, "I wonder what Grandma Althea's going to send me this year?"

Penny and Dan exchanged a long meaningful look, while Tiffany rolled her big brown eyes up toward the ceiling. Grandma Althea's gifts were always exotic, interesting, different, surprising, and unpredictable. They were magic, like her.

Reinaldo was just a baby when his grandmother Althea, his mom's mom, went off to live in Nepal , a country so far away it was pretty much on the other side of the world. She wanted to live in a simple place where people worshipped God all day long, she said, not just once a week.

Althea had always been different from other people. She laughed more, and she didn't care if her dishes all matched or if her clothes were fashionable, which they weren't. All that seemed funny to her. She believed in two things that Reinaldo knew about. She believed in magic and she believed in love. Sometimes in his dreams, he would hear her whisper to him, "and I don't think there's any difference between the two."

When Reinaldo was just a baby, he got little Nepalese baby clothes as presents. There was a royal looking purple silk baby gown trimmed in gold that Penny put on him once and took a picture to send to Althea. After that it was wrapped in tissue paper and stored in a trunk. Then he got a little hand woven

4

hat and jacket, very soft and warm from the fuzzy undercoat of a mountain goat. He got to wear that all winter long, and always felt so cozy and safe in it. There were toys, little tin boats with candles in them that you lit to make them chug chug chug around the bathtub, wooden tops and hand-carved puppets. They sat on a shelf in his room, next to all the brightly colored plastic toys that everyone else gave him. It was his Tibetan toy shelf, since his grandma told him most of them were made by refugees from Tibet. On his 5th birthday, Reinaldo got stars to paste on his walls.

"Ridiculous!" exclaimed Penny, "We've just painted his room, and these will ruin the paint job!" (His walls had just been painted, not the deep dark blue he asked for, but a soft pale blue that his parents liked better.) That night, when the house was quiet and it seemed like everyone was asleep, Reinaldo took his little package of stars out of the drawer and looked at them. Even by the dim night-light, they glowed with a golden light, and pulsated in their pretty cellophane package. "It couldn't hurt," he thought, "to just put up a couple. I'll put them where Mom won't see them, so she won't get upset." But when he tore the package open, the stars flew out, on their own, and landed all over his ceiling and walls, until it was like sleeping outside on a beautiful starry night. It was so magical, he forgot to even worry what his mom would say.

The next morning when Penny came to wake him up for school, she didn't say anything but, "Wake up sweetie. It's time to get up." He could see the stars, on the blue walls that seemed darker than the day before. "It looks to me like your walls have gotten a little darker," she said. "We should never buy paint on sale. Well, come on now, get up..." and she left the room with a slightly puzzled look on her face. Magic. He knew it.

His sixth birthday present was a stick. It was a fancy looking stick with a thick glass bubble at one end, all wrapped in silk and tied with ribbons. Interesting. It got set aside while Reinaldo busied himself with big toy trucks and new books, birthday cake and friends. But when he went to his room, hours later, he took out the stick to study it. As he held it in his hand, the blue bubble of glass began to glow and send out a warm light.

A few days later Reinaldo got a chance to find out what the stick was. It wasn't a magic wand like a Halloween abracadabra magic wand that would turn butterflies into prancing ponies and bad grades into A's. It was a real life danger detector with reactive warning signals: whenever danger was near, the wand reacted. Mild danger, like his mom in a bad mood or a rainstorm coming when he was blocks from home, made the bubble glow softly and give off a little gurgle, just to get his attention. As the danger got bigger, the wand reacted stronger, glowing bright and hot and positively buzzing in his hand. The hottest it ever got was when he went with his mom to the bank just as a bank robber went in there, too. The wand glowed hot and bright, especially when Reinaldo was facing a scowling, angry looking man who had his hand on something in his pocket.

"I'll show them," the would-be bank robber was muttering under his breath. "I'll be rich and then..." but his thoughts trailed off. A warm glowing light had caught his eye, coming from a little boy in the next line. As he stared at it, he woke up all of a sudden, like a bubble popping. "What do I think I'm doing???" he asked himself, and no one else in particular. "I must be *nuts!*" And he turned on his heel and walked out of the bank. The light of the wand flickered, then went out. That was the first time Reinaldo realized he had an authentic danger detector that could turn bad thoughts to good. Or at least improve them.

A few days later, Billy Mulcaney wanted to pick a fight with Reinaldo over nothing, just because he was twice Reinaldo's size so he figured he could beat him, no problem. Reinaldo just turned slightly so the wand, buzzing softly, was aimed at Billy. "Uh, I uh wanted to ask you something," said Billy with a more confused look on his face than usual, "but now I can't remember what it was." He walked away looking truly perplexed, and hadn't bothered Reinaldo since.

Funny, but the wand didn't work so well on Penny and Dan and Tiffany. Sure, at first, they got cheerful and had fun whenever Reinaldo pointed it their way. But after awhile, they just got used to it. Since he didn't know if it was a lifetime wand, or just good for a limited number of interventions, Reinaldo didn't want to use it up on everyday bad moods and crankiness. He carried it with him all the time, but didn't aim it at anything below a soft buzz. A simple glow wasn't worth risking using it up!

His seventh birthday was rainy and chilly. It just happened to fall on a Saturday, and there was going to be a party that afternoon with some of his friends from school. Penny wanted it to be special, so to surprise Reinaldo, she had hired a magician, Arsene the Illusionist, to do a show for the kids. Sure, it was extravagant, but Reinaldo loved magic so much, and you only turn seven once.

All morning, Reinaldo listened for the doorbell. Surely his grandmother wouldn't miss his birthday! His birthday present had always arrived just exactly on the day of the birthday, unless it fell on a Sunday, in which case it came on Saturday. Penny and Dan would talk about it in hushed tones, "How does she get it here right on time, every time? She has to walk down the mountain to the village, and find a truck that's going to the city. Then it has to get on a plane to the States. Once it gets here, it's UPS or the post office. How does she get it here right on time?" But Reinaldo knew how. His grandma was magic.

When the doorbell rang, Reinaldo ran to get it. It was his friend Wally Brian who lived next door and usually came early, so they could plan and dream and talk about which would be the best presents to get. In all the excitement, Reinaldo stopped wondering about his grandmother's gift.

His party was really fun. There were games and prizes, balloons and cake, friends laughing and having a good time together. But the best part of all was the visit from Arsene the Illusionist.

First he juggled, then he took coins out of peoples ears, and out of their hair. He made balls disappear in mid-air, and then he pulled them out of

Morty Rosenwieg's nose! He took a flower out of thin air and put it in Urmi Rao's hair, then reached down his sleeve and pulled out a rabbit. It was so soft and sniffy and the kids all wanted to pat it. Just as they did, Waffles ran into the room, way too interested in the furry little creature. Poof! It disappeared! Reinaldo hoped Arsene wouldn't pull the rabbit out of *his* nose, or make Waffles disappear too! Maybe he wouldn't practice that disappearing trick with Waffles, after all!

Finally, it was time to go. The magician gathered up his things, which all fit nicely into a little black case, then, wrapping his black magician's cape around his shoulders, bowed low.

"Ah yes," he said, the light from his eyes twinkling, making Reinaldo feel warm and happy inside, "I nearly forgot my most important trick."

He clapped his hands together and a flame appeared. Reaching down into the flame, with everyone gasping in disbelief, he pulled at something long and black and shiny. The flames licked at it, and at his hands, but nothing burned. Then poof! again: the flame went out, and in his hands, Arsene held the most beautiful black silk cape, with gold silk on the inside, and embroidered on the back, in shining gold thread the words:

Reinaldo the Magnificent

"Your Grandmother Althea asked me to tell you Happy Birthday" he smiled at Reinaldo, whose eyes were shining bright and big as saucers. And with a swirl and a whoosh, Arsene was gone.

That night, Reinaldo had a dream about a small brown-skinned man in a dark brown robe. His boots and robe were made of thick, hand-tanned suede with symbols embroidered all over them. The man crinkled his eyes, smiled and put his finger to his lips. "Hush," was the message as he reached down into his robe and pulled out a long shiny banner of black silk. "Gramma say happy burrday," was all he said, then turned and was gone in a flash. Reinaldo knew it was a magic dream, sent to him by his grandmother. It was one of her favorite ways of keeping in touch, although why she sent the little man, instead of coming herself, was a mystery.

Grandma Althea

Althea hadn't always lived so far away. Before Reinaldo was born, she lived for months with Penny and Dan and Tiffany, helping Penny take care of the family while Dan worked at his job. When Reinaldo was a year old, Althea left on a trip looking for a new home, where she felt like she really fit in. Even though she loved Penny, Dan, and Tiffany, she was getting tired of living with them. She didn't think like them or believe what they did or want to live like them. She wanted to live where she felt free to be herself, just as she really was.

When Reinaldo was born, Penny named him Reiner. Nobody knew where she got that name, but everybody loved it. And then Althea started calling him Baby Reinaldo, and there it was. The name stuck and he'd been Reinaldo ever since. Even his teachers called him that, except for old Mrs. Humphries who taught third grade and hadn't laughed in about a hundred years. She would shake her blubbery jaw at him and roar, "Reiner!" just to make a point that she was not going to call him Reinaldo. But everyone else did.

Althea was named after her grandmother, who came from England and taught her about fairies and elves and magic. She tried to be like the other girls, wearing makeup and going out with football players, but the thing was, she knew about fairies and elves and magic. When she went to college, she married a handsome football player who won her heart with his good looks and his good sense of humor. Then he changed; he just got mean.

He was always cranky and tired, angry at someone or angry about something. Althea would try to cheer him up, but it was never good enough. If she bought tickets to a special event for them, he said she paid too much. If she cooked a wonderful dinner for him, it was always overcooked, or not cooked enough. If she bought herself some new clothes to look pretty, he said she wasted all their money. If she didn't, he told her she didn't take care of herself and she looked old. She thought after Penny was born, he'd sweeten up, but he didn't.

After a while, Althea had had enough. She took her clothes, baby Penny, and got on the train back to her parents' farm. Her mom took care of

Penny while Althea went back to college so she could get a good job. Penny loved her grandparents, strict old people who believed in hard work. She became serious and quiet with them, and listened carefully to their advice.

"Work hard and save your money," they would tell her. "You never want to be in a mess like your mother, not having enough money."

Althea loved going to college, and as soon as she graduated, she got a job as a librarian in their little town. It was a wonderful job because she got to be with two things she loved the most: books and people. She earned enough money to rent a cozy little apartment just for herself and Penny. Sure, sometimes it was hard being a single mom, but her parents helped. And when she picked Penny up after school   and went home to their little apartment, there was nobody grouchy or angry there. Althea could laugh and dance and sing if she wanted to, with only Penny to stare at her in amazement.

After Penny grew up, and went off to college and got married and moved into a home of her own, Althea didn't have to be serious *at all* anymore. She let her hair grow long and curly and gray, like a big tangled cloud. She started wearing big dangly earrings, and bright colored clothes that looked to the townspeople like gypsy clothes. Even though some people thought she was getting old (certainly old enough to settle down!) Althea felt young and free. One day she called Penny to tell her she was going on a trip for awhile, and could she store a few things in her attic? She had already quit her job and bought a round-the-world plane ticket.

"Mother, what in the *world* are you doing?" asked Penny, appalled that her mother would fly off with no plan and no known destination. Her tendency to wear wild clothing and say wild things, believe in magic and not care about anything proper was almost more than Penny could bear. She was glad, in a way, that her mother was leaving, because Tiffany was nearly six years old and she wasn't sure she wanted her mother as an influence.

But when Althea came back from her travels a year later, Penny was pregnant with Reinaldo and not feeling very well at all. She could barely drag herself out of bed every day, much less take care of her little family. The day Althea arrived, she had to catch a shuttle from the airport. Penny couldn't pick her up. She was just too sick, and Dan was at work.

Althea came to the house and couldn't believe her eyes. The house that had always been so spotless and neat was a wreck. Dirty dishes were piled high in the sink and down the kitchen counters. The garbage can was full of instant food containers. Dirty laundry was piled by the washer, and clean laundry was piled on the guest bed. It was all Penny could do to get it there. Folding it was out of the question.

Penny came to the door, hugged Althea, said "Hi Mom, I'm glad you're here," and ran to the bathroom to throw up again. "Whew", thought Althea, "that must be some strong little baby to get her that sick!"

So Althea stayed. The house got cleaned and the laundry got done. Penny slept and slept and stopped throwing up. Dan came home happy to find a clean house and a well-rested wife, a happy family and a great dinner on the table. Although he would have liked more meat, he had to admit the food was really tasty. Althea planted a little vegetable garden and made them wonderful meals with the food she grew.

When Reinaldo was born, Althea knew right away that he was different. He was small, and dark. When she was a child, they would have said he was a gypsy. From the very first day, he followed her with his bright, dark eyes. People who looked at him said, "what a little old man, " or "what an old soul." She felt herself falling so in love with him that she didn't know what she would do when she had to go.

But she knew she'd have to go. There was no doubt about it. Penny was strong now, and wanted to be in charge in her own home again. And besides, Althea had to be neat and all tucked in, and it was cramping her style. She started wearing sweat suits and sneakers instead of the long skirts and bright tunics that she loved. Her wild long hair was always tied up when she went to the store, or the bank. She hung up her big hoop earrings and wore little simple ones. But people still stared, as they had for years, because no matter what she did, there was just something different about her. She glowed from inside. Althea wanted to travel again and live in a place where she felt free to be herself.

Reinaldo had his name and her heart. If she didn't leave soon, she wouldn't be able to at all. With tears in her eyes, she packed, not planning to be gone for so long, caught in the gentle rhythm of a life with no hours or rules, no clocks or telephones. She knew where she was going: back to the little mountain village in Nepal that she had visited the year before.

First, she took a plane as far as you could go by plane, then a bus to the end of the line. From there she caught a ride in a truck up to the little mountain village that she liked so well. Outside the village, up on the mountain, stood a little mud house, all alone. The old people who had lived there had died, and their children had gone to the city to work. It was hers to live in, if she wanted it. She could rent it for so little money it was easy.

She had left all her sweat suits behind, packed up at Penny and Dan's with her hair bands and watches. Instead, she wore the robes the mountain people wore. In the summers she wore light, bright robes to keep out the heat, and in the fierce mountain winters, piled on wool robes and thick suede boots and outer robes. They were simple and beautiful, embroidered all over with symbols of love and magic. And that was where she met Tenzin, the man of her dreams. And more recently, in Reinaldo's dream, too.

Tenzin had left Tibet years before, when the Chinese invaded his country. He was not a monk, although his brothers were and he knew many. He lived alone on a mountainside, and kept goats for his living. He had had a wife once, but she had died one night, before all the troubles started and he had to move. It was a blessing that she was spared the heartache of having to leave their home. Maybe it was a blessing for her, but he missed her terribly. Until he met Althea.

One morning, Althea was sitting outside her little house when a sprightly man in Tibetan robes rounded the bend, leading his little band of goats to graze. He caught her eye, and a beam of light passed between them; they felt like they knew each other at once. Over time, Althea taught Tenzin a few English words, and he taught her enough Tibetan so they could have a simple conversation, but they didn't really need to talk much. They could be together all day, not talking, and feel the space had been full.

After she had lived there for a few years, tourists with a camera came through Althea's village. They wanted to take pictures of her; well, they wanted to take pictures of everything. She made them a deal.

"I'll be glad to help you with your picture taking," she told them. "But I would like a favor from you in return. Please take a picture of me outside my house and send it to my grandson, Reinaldo. I will give you his address."

The tourists were delighted. All day long, they traveled around with Althea. She talked to the people as best she could, in simple Nepalese words and sign language to tell them what the camera did. She helped the tourists get the pictures they wanted. There were pictures of women weaving the long goat hair into strong wool cloth, of children reciting their lessons, and of the young boys bringing the goats home in the evening. There were pictures of the famous 107 year old man on his horse, and of beautiful green terraces of tea growing on the mountainsides. And there was a picture of Althea, the one that sits by Reinaldo's bed.

In it, she is standing on a mountainside in front of a small house made of mud, with a red tile roof. The trees on the mountainside are small, and bent with the wind. The mountainside is so bare, it looks like there are more rocks than plants. The wind must be strong because Althea's long curly hair is blowing back so you can really see her face. Her eyes are so bright and intense, they seem alive, and her mouth is curled up at the edges in the happiest most contented looking smile. Around her neck hangs a cord with a huge glowing red amulet on the end, and then several smaller cords holding different shining stones and pieces of handmade jewelry. Her clothes are long robes that billow in the wind. She is brown and healthy and she looks very peaceful and happy.

On Reinaldo's fourth birthday, the photo arrived from some strangers in Germany, the same exact day that the little tin boats and a soft warm goat wool blanket arrived from Nepal.

The Birthday Wish

"Eight years old," Reinaldo was chanting to himself as he and Waffles did a magic dance around the bedroom. "Eight years old and I wanna wanna new bike and a new computer game." They did the wiggle dance, Waffles jumping up and trying to dance on his own hind legs. But the trouble was, Reinaldo already *had* a bike, and he had a lot of computer games. He had a ton of clothes and he even had his own TV, even though it was a little one that he almost never watched.

At dinner, Penny and Dan had quizzed him about what he wanted for his birthday, and what kind of party he wanted. Even Tiffany, momentarily distracted from thinking about her hair and her face, asked him what he would like, since she had been saving her allowance to buy him a present. It was really hard to think of something, and besides, it felt like they were trying to keep the subject away from Althea's present, whatever *that* turned out to be!

Lying in bed that night, Reinaldo looked around his room. The walls had turned a deep nighttime blue, and the stars, which no one in his family could see but him, shone brightly all around him. His magic wand lay quietly on the night table, humming softly as it did at night to recharge itself. He was snuggled under his goat wool blanket, now worn with age, with his cape spread over the top. He turned his head to say goodnight to Althea, as he did every night for nearly four years, when all of a sudden he *knew* what he wanted for his birthday more than anything in the world.

"Grandma, I want you to come see me. I haven't seen you in this whole life except when I was a baby, and I don't remember you. Please please please come see me for my birthday." He could almost swear he saw her wink, and then, he fell asleep.

Half a world away, in a little house on a mountainside in the kingdom of Nepal, a fire blazed up on the hearth and Althea heard his prayer. "Oh dear," she whispered to herself. "I didn't want to go back so soon. If only he hadn't said that third "please'."

There's an old saying "three's a charm." It has been true a long time. Say something three times, and you give it power. "Please, please, please" went straight to Althea's heart. Yes, it was time to visit her grandson, and the rest of the family too, of course, although they had never had much in common. She still loved them dearly, but she didn't miss them like she did Reinaldo. She sat and stared into the fire, and then fed it the little bits of wood and pine-cones she had gathered on the hillside. As it blazed merrily, she looked around her tiny little house.

It was only one room, with a bed in the corner and the hearth, where she cooked and kept warm. Shower? Don't make me laugh! Her bathtub was a big metal tub she filled with hot water when she wanted a bath. It was hard work. She had to carry the water in pails up the mountain from a well below the house, then put it on the fire to heat. At first, it had seemed so hard. Now, she was strong, and used to it.

The only light in the house was from the fire. Althea hadn't lit her kerosene lantern even though it was still dark in the house; Reinaldo's bedtime was about time for her to get up, being halfway around the world.

The flames danced and reflected gently on the whitewashed walls. Less than three days, and she would be gone. It felt right, but it felt sad, too. This house had been such a sacred place for her: she had arrived a sad and lonely grandmother, aching for her grandson. In the seven years she had been here, she had learned to be quiet and live with the rhythms of the mountains.

When the sun rose, the bleating of Tenzin's goats going out to graze would wake her up. On fine sunny days, she might sit for hours, watching a hawk hunting way up in the mountains, or go with Tenzin up the mountain, following the goats as they searched for food on the barren hillside. Sometimes she sat still, just watching the clouds and listening to the wind. In this way, she became peaceful. Thinking about heading back into the land of TV's and telephones didn't really thrill her (and she didn't even know yet about cell phones and computers in just about every home!!!)

But Reinaldo had said "please, please, please!" It was the message she had been expecting, almost waiting for. Besides, seven years was a full cycle. It was time to go. Tenzin would understand, and she would need his help. There was a lot of powerful magic needed to get her there in less than three days, if she was going to make it for his birthday!

Homecoming

In the clear blue light of morning, Reinaldo opened his eyes. "What was that?" It was his birthday, and he was eight years old today. It was awfully quiet in the house....it must be really early. Waffles muttered under the covers, where he was *not* supposed to be, and twitched and jerked, chasing a dream rabbit, or getting chased by a mean dream dog. Reinaldo couldn't tell which, but he figured that must have been what he heard.

He thought about his parents, and how freaked out they were when he said the only thing he wanted for his birthday was for his grandma to come see him. They looked so concerned; they knew it couldn't happen. She was half a world away, and hadn't called or written or anything to say she was coming. They knew it was impossible. A birthday party would have been just the thing to help with the disappointment they knew he would face at the end of the day, but Reinaldo had insisted. His grandma was coming. He could feel it.

"Move over, Waffles." He gave the little dog a friendly shove with his leg. Waffles was so little, but he always took up more than half the bed. Reinaldo was sure being squished against the wall had woken him up, too, so he wiggled down into his covers, claiming the most territory he could. "Reinaldo...." he heard it more clearly this time. Someone was calling his name, so quietly he didn't know if he was really hearing it, or hearing it inside, in his heart.

Sitting up, he looked out the window. Out on the lawn stood a little woman wrapped in robes and sparkling jewels. Her hair was loose and curly, and on her feet she wore the most curious pair of boots, covered in symbols.

"Grandma," Reinaldo fairly screamed and went racing down the stairs, Waffles a puzzled but willing step behind him. "Grandma," he said again, more softly as he opened the front door and saw her standing right there. "Grandma," he barely whispered as she wrapped her arms around him and held him in the warmest, softest, safest, lovingest seven-years-in-the-making hug.

"Reinaldo", she whispered back, her eyes wet with happy tears, "you have become such a big boy. Reinaldo the Magnificent." And holding each other's hands, they went back into the house, Waffles trotting happily between them as if he had known Althea all his life, instead of just having met her. "Ah...." she exclaimed with a big smile that crinkled her eyes and made them dance, "this must be the famous Waffles." As she bent down to hug him, Waffles wiggled and wagged so hard, it looked like he'd come out of his skin. He instantly loved her as much as Reinaldo did.

Penny and Dan woke up later to a wonderful smell and the sound of soft laughter and giggles coming from the kitchen. They looked at each other in surprise. Surely Tiffany hadn't gotten up and made breakfast? She was always the *last* one up on weekends. And Reinaldo didn't really know how to cook breakfast, since he usually got himself a bowl of cereal and a banana if he got up early. But that smell, it was so familiar, vanilla and butter and........

"Oh my gosh!" Penny shouted, "My mother's here!!!"

Grabbing a robe and tying it around her as she raced down the hall, Penny burst into the kitchen and straight into her mother's open arms.

"Mom!" she whispered, her face full of tears and Althea's curls, "How did you get here? Why didn't you let us know?......." But Althea only smiled and hugged her only child, patting her hair as if Penny were a little girl again.

The kitchen seemed to glow by the time Dan got in there, a few minutes behind Penny. He had stopped long enough to brush his teeth, since Tiffany had told him quite clearly what a kiss from his unbrushed lips was like in the morning. (Kissing an evil toad that will never turn into a prince.) He and Althea hugged and kissed, and told each other how happy they were to see each other. All of a sudden, Dan and Penny both remembered at the same time. They spun around and grinned at Reinaldo. "Hey Sweetheart, Happy Birthday" and "Happy Birthday, Sport!" You can guess, I bet, who said what...

"And we're having birthday cakes early!" grinned Reinaldo excitedly, "Pancakes." That was the delicious smell! Althea's famous pancakes, made with just enough vanilla and cinnamon to make them so yummy you couldn't stop eating them, and make the house smell great for hours. Warm butter melted into maple syrup, with spiced coffee (that always smelled much better than it tasted) and hot cocoa. Everyone was so happy and full, it was like a birthday party just being at breakfast. Only someone was missing.... and not Waffles, who was eating his pancake with just butter, thank you, since sweets are not good for dogs, from his little dish by the door.

"Grandma!!" Tiffany leaned against the door jam, a goofy grin on her face. Her hair was all a mess, not combed or sprayed, and she didn't have on her makeup or her glamour girl look. She looked totally cute in her flannel jammies and her bunny slippers. Like the sweet girl she really was, when she wasn't pretending to be somebody else.

Althea got up from the table and took her in her arms for a big hug. It really was good to be home.

"Mom, where's your luggage?" Penny asked Althea when breakfast was over.

"I just brought one small bag, so I could carry it myself," Althea told her. "The rest will come later." Of course she didn't tell how it would arrive, whether by magic or standard shipping, and nobody asked. Reinaldo didn't ask because he didn't need to, and the rest of the family didn't want to know!

"We'll put you in your old room, if that's ok?" Penny asked her and was answered by Althea's smile. "Only you need to know that it's become the computer room since you left."

"You're kidding! No, I can see you're not kidding." Althea's eyes were wide with surprise. A computer room? She knew about computers, of course, but Penny and Dan? What were they doing with one?

"Grandma, everybody has a computer. Almost everyone at school has one. We do our homework on them and play video games and go on the Internet and look for stuff." Tiffany looked at her a little like she was from Mars, but Tiffany looked at everyone like that, at one point or another. Anyway, in Althea's case, she practically was from Mars, at least for the last seven years.

But when she thought about it, learning to use a computer would be really fun. She could show the kids all about Nepal and her life there, from the comfort of their own home. They wouldn't have to take a truck up a muddy mountain road, if they could find pictures of her little village, which was really tiny.

This was magic of a different kind. They could sit in the house and visit the whole world, see

27

pictures, even zoom in and see her house, if they could find the village. Even though most people were used to computers, Althea wasn't. Having one to use was something brand new in her life. This was going to be fun!

Dan's Big Surprise

"C'mon Dad!" Reinaldo yelled excitedly. They were more than halfway up Overlook Mountain, and Reinaldo was impatient to get to the top. Up ahead, he could see Althea sitting quietly on a rock, watching the hawks, circling below. Reinaldo wanted to get up there with her. That was the coolest thing, to be able to sit so high up a mountain that you looked down on the clouds and the birds. Reinaldo had only been here once before, on a school trip. This time it was a special birthday wish that they all go to the top of the mountain together. Penny and Tiffany had stopped to look at wildflowers, but the path was so well marked, they agreed to all meet at the top.

"C'mon Dad!" Reinaldo called again. Dan just raised his face and gave him a blank look. His face was a weird, grayish color. And then he collapsed, crumpling to the ground.

"GRANDMA!!!!!" Reinaldo screamed as he tore down the mountain to his dad. He did a baseball slide to Dan's side and loosened Dan's jacket from around his throat. Althea was right behind him, running faster than he thought a grandma could, lifting Dan's head gently and cradling it in her lap. Just then Tiffany and Penny came into view, and the sight of the other three, Dan all gray and limp, with Althea holding him and Reinaldo dancing around him in distress, got them running. Luckily for them all, but most of all for Dan, Tiffany never traveled anywhere without her handy cell phone in her little lavender backpack. She dialed 911 and handed it to her mother.

Within minutes, the sound of a helicopter could be heard. There was a clearing up near the mountain top. The paramedics scrambled down with a stretcher and just minutes later, the 'copter lifted off with Dan on a stretcher, and Penny by his side. Even though Reinaldo would have given *anything* to ride in a helicopter, he had the good sense not to ask. This was looking way too serious, and scary. Penny's face was drained of color, but the medics acted really calm and assured her it would all be fine. Althea called to her, "We'll meet you at the hospital...."

So down the hill they ran, into the next adventure of Althea's first time driving in over seven years "Nothin' to it" she grinned, wheeling the car around the curves, heading downhill, down the mountain to town, down down down to the hospital in the middle of town. And all the way there, she made them breathe.

Everybody breathes all the time, but most people take shallow little breaths up in the top of their lungs. Althea had learned to BREATHE, all the way down into her belly. It's what pushed her up and down the mountain so fast, and what kept her so calm. All the way to the hospital, she had Reinaldo and Tiffany practice. No talking, no wondering if their dad was ok and worrying about him.

"If you can, send him lots of love and light," she told them. "Don't send him fears and worries. He doesn't need those!"

Pulling right up to the emergency room and parking, Althea turned to Reinaldo and Tiffany. "Now remember what I told you. Breathe. Nice deep breaths. It will help you stay calm, and that will help your parents right now. They're probably scared and they need you to be as strong as you can." Then all three ran into the emergency room hall. Empty! Where was everyone???

Just then a young technician came out of an examining room. "Whoa there," he gave them a smile, slowing down their mad dash down the hall, "can I help you?"

"We're looking for Dan Parkerman," Althea told him. "He was brought in by helicopter........"

"Come with me," the young tech said, and then added, "He's going to be ok. I'll take you to his room."

With that, Tiffany burst into tears. She had been so scared that her dad would die, he looked so awful. She was thinking about all the times he wanted her to help, and she wouldn't, or watch something on TV with him, and she wouldn't, or just be nice to be around, and she wouldn't. In her heart, she had been praying and praying, "Just let him be ok, and I'll change, God, I promise. I'll be nicer, and I'll help, just please don't let him die."

Penny and the doctor were talking when the three others came into Dan's room. He was lying in the bed, looking pretty worn out but at least he wasn't that awful gray color anymore. Penny introduced her family to the doctor, "This is my mother Althea, my daughter Tiffany, come here darling, Daddy's ok, and my son, Reinaldo, who turned eight years old today. We were celebrating his birthday with a hike up Overlook. This is Doctor Richards. He says Dad will be fine."

Doctor Richards was pretty young, too, for a doctor. At least, he looked young. He was tall, and tan, and looked like he could run up and down Overlook Mountain with no problem. And he BREATHED. You could see just watching him how relaxed he stayed, even when he was in the middle of a crisis. He gave Reinaldo a wink, "Good birthday wish, except your dad hasn't been hiking enough lately and it put a strain on his heart."

He saw Reinaldo's look, and instantly reassured him. "Please don't feel like you did this to your dad. He's really lucky because he got a wake up call like this. Many people just keep going and out of the blue have a full-scale heart attack. He had what we call ventricular tachycardia. All it means is that his heart got pushed harder than it was used to."

It was hard to accept, but in a way, that was a kind of magic too, that Dan got such a big wake up call before he had a real heart attack, only it wasn't the kind of magic Reinaldo wanted much of!

Penny and Dan had already heard the doctor's diagnosis, and thought they knew what was coming next. Diet and exercise. What they didn't expect was that Dr. Richards would get the whole family to help.

"Hey," he told Reinaldo and Tiffany, "I know a way you can help, if you want to?" He looked over their heads at Penny, who gave him a nod that said, "Go for it, whatever it is."

"You," he said, looking at Tiffany, "can go for a walk with your dad every evening when he gets home from work. Just 10 minutes or so, until he gets used to it. Think you can do that?" Tiffany was just about to roll her eyes, like the old Tiffany, when she remembered her pledge. "Sure, I'd like that. It'll give us time together to talk." Dan almost had a real heart attack when he heard that, and he almost started crying, too. He had really missed his little girl, since she became Miss Glamourpuss.

"And you, birthday boy," smiled the doctor, who everyone was liking more and more, "I want you to make sure there is no junk food in the house, and get your dad to practice some ball with you when he's had a little time to recuperate." Reinaldo thought about that unused basketball hoop in the driveway. "You bet!!"

Then both kids shyly went over to their dad's bed, one on each side, not sure of what they could say or do since he was a hospital patient. But he opened his arms wide and hugged them to him, holding them close, and whispering, "I love you more than anything," into their hair as he thanked God for letting him have another chance.

A Whole New Life

Nothing in the house was the same after that. Dan stayed in the hospital another day, and Penny was there every second she had. She still went to work, but she went straight to the hospital right after. It was a good thing Grandma was around! She cooked, and kept the house together. When Penny got home, the house was calm and quiet.

When Dan came home, he had to rest for a week. Tiffany, Reinaldo, Waffles and Althea would hang out in the kitchen, making dinner together and BREATHING. They talked about their days, and what they learned in school. It was really peaceful being together, if you count laughing as peaceful.

First Althea would surprise them with some story from her life in Nepal, then Tiffany would shock her with some story from school. They couldn't quite believe her world was real, and she couldn't quite believe their world, full of all kinds of scary things.

One thing Grandma really liked about this "new" world was the Internet. She could see it now. If she lived near a telephone line, she could go online and be in touch with her grandchildren any time after she went home to Nepal. She was dreaming more and more about going back. She missed Tenzin, and also, there was the issue of the television.

In Althea's little mud house in Nepal, there was no television. There was also no phone, and no computer, or anything else like that, because there was no electricity. Down in the village there was a TV in the general store that had the electric line to it, but mostly what it showed was wavy lines and grackle. Althea liked to sit in silence, like Tenzin had taught her. But Penny and Dan really got into TV. Dan watched the news, which Althea called "the bad news," since they never showed all the wonderful things people did for each other all over the world every day. Nope, it was one bad, mean, ugly story after another, and Althea didn't like to watch it or hear it or have it in her brain all day unless it was something she really needed to know.

And just as bad as the news was the advertising. Tiffany and Reinaldo couldn't believe that Grandma lived in a place with no electricity or running water, which automatically meant no TV or VCR or computers, because there was no phone either, and no microwave ovens or even toaster ovens or refrigerators.

Mornings had become Althea's most favorite time. Before the sun rose, while the world lay still and quiet, Althea would get out of her bed in the computer room, light some candles and wave a stick of incense, to clear her sleep away, to clear the air. After she went to the bathroom and washed her face and brushed her teeth, she would sit on her meditation cushion, wrapped in a big soft shawl that looked like a blue cloud. When she closed her eyes, she got drawn into a huge still pool of silence, and after she sat there awhile, sometimes she got messages from Tenzin. She missed him and his nutty sense of humor. This was the best way to keep in touch, since he didn't have a phone or email either.

And then a bell would ring, an alarm clock. In her mountain house she went to sleep when the sun went down, and got up just before it did. Here, everyone's life had these complicated schedules: Penny had to be at her job at the bank by 8:30, only most of the time there was more work to do than she had time for so she went even earlier. Dan didn't have to get to work until 9, but since he had to travel farther, it was about the same. Tiffany went to the high school, which started at 8, but Reinaldo went to the elementary school, which didn't start until 8:45. Sometimes they took the school bus, sometimes Dan drove the kids to school, and sometimes Penny drove Tiffany and Dan drove Reinaldo. Whew! Althea was happy to stay home with Waffles and putter around the house, work in the little garden and cook wonderful treats for the family to enjoy when they got home.

Every evening, Tiffany and Dan went for a walk and talked about what had happened that day, and what they thought and felt about it. For the first time since Tiffany was really small, before Dan got so buried in his work and Tiffany in her glamour magazines, they became close again. And Reinaldo found out his ol' dad could still teach him a thing or two about basketball. When the weather was warm, they'd go out after dinner and play until dark, feinting and jabbing down the driveway, making those big Championship moves, laughing and pushing each other like it was really a big competition, with money riding on it. The only one who seemed to be missing out on all the family fun was Penny.

Her job at the bank was stressful. Reinaldo didn't understand it very well, and Tiffany didn't try, but there was something about the interest rates going down, so everybody was at the bank borrowing money. Or something. They all knew one thing: Penny was working way too many hours, and coming home exhausted and cranky, to eat and fall in bed and do it again the next day. She was even working on Saturdays now, and even though the bank had PROMISED it would only be for a couple of weeks, it was already becoming a big problem. If Grandma wasn't there they would be eating frozen dinners again, or worse, their own cooking!

One Friday night, Penny didn't get home until nearly ten o'clock, and when she came in the door, she started to cry. She had missed going out for pizza with the family, and then they had gone to the movies. Everyone was having fun but her. Dan had certainly changed *his* habits since his little heart attack; he was spending more time than ever with the kids, and taking better care of himself than he had since college. He took Penny in his big arms and hugged her, but that only made her cry more. Reinaldo and Tiffany looked worried, and Althea ran into the kitchen to make a hot cup of tea for her poor, weary daughter.

They all sat at the table while Penny had her tea, then some yummy oatmeal cookies Grandma Althea had made that afternoon, then a bowl of soup and some toast and pretty soon she was almost as good as new. Her hand flew to her mouth, "Oh No! It's nearly 11 and I have to be at work by 8 tomorrow!" Dan stared at her in disbelief. Reinaldo and Tiffany's faces fell, and even Althea, who tried never to say anything that wasn't positive and supportive, hugged Penny and said, "Oh honey, do you really *have to*?"

There was a weird, thick kind of silence in the room. Everybody wanted to support Penny, who was having a hard enough time, but also wanted to scream at her, "Stop it!!! Stay home with us. We're your family and we love you and need you." They all had those thoughts in their heads, but of course they didn't say them. One look at her drawn, tired face made them realize they couldn't. Only Dan had one more thing to say. "Honey," he said, looking at Penny, "on Sunday, I'd like to go for a ride in the country just with you. We've got some stuff to figure out."

Sunday was a great day. It dawned clear and cool, but not too cold to be outside. Tiffany, Reinaldo and Althea packed a basket full of food, sandwiches and cookies and fruit and Milk Bones ('cause of course Waffles was going, too) and took off to hike and eat their lunch on the top of Overlook Mountain. It was going to be cold at the top, so they took their backpacks, with blankets and jackets, and had the best day, exploring among the rocks, and watching the hawks soaring. Althea felt such a pang in her heart, watching the hawks. She even imagined that she saw some prayer flags flapping in the breeze, down in the little hidden valley on the wilderness side of the mountain. It reminded her of her mountain village, and Tenzin. Even though she felt so happy with her family, and especially with her grandchildren, she longed to see Tenzin again, and sit in his funny silence, just watching him as he fixed something and chuckled to himself. Yes, she missed him very much.

Meanwhile, Dan and Penny took another route. She was much too tired for anything as hard as hiking, so they drove to a peaceful spot on the lake that they had loved so much when they first got together. "Remember all the times we came out here, just to get away together and have some peace and quiet?" Penny nodded. It had been so long since they had just taken a time-out together. They got out of the car and walked slowly along the shore of the lake. It was cold enough to have the place to themselves, and that suited them just fine. Peace and quiet was exactly what they needed.

"Pen, I can't stand it seeing you so tired out. I don't think I can take much more of it, and I don't want to. Life is too short for this."

"I know Dan. I miss the kids, I miss you, I miss feeling normal and having a life. I feel like all I do is work, work, work."

"Well, today we're gonna figure this out and come up with some other way to work things. But first, I think we need to find a place to have lunch."

They walked back to the car, slowly, looking at all the trees changing their colors and watching the geese out on the lake. As Penny slowed down, the bank was far from her thoughts. Time with her husband was precious, and time with the kids and her mom was precious, and she was losing all that. She had to figure something out!!!

Yvonne's Rest Stop and Grill was just the kind of place they needed to feed their bodies and souls. Yvonne was an elderly French woman who had lived in the area for thirty years. She knew where to find the best wild berries and who sold the freshest eggs. She made her own bread and wild berry pies, and soups from her garden and fish from the lake. Penny had always looked at her in amazement: how could this old woman do so much? Everything was always delicious and made you feel good inside. Even the food made Penny see how stressed and wired she was, because it was so simple and pure and wonderful. And then, right there and all of a sudden, Penny made a decision.

"I am going to leave the bank. I'm not quite sure yet what I'll do, but I want to do something I love, and I want to be there for my family. I hadn't even realized how unfair this has been to my mom. She's doing my job, when all she did was come for a visit."

Dan patted her hand. He didn't have to say much, but he was a happy man.

All the way home, Penny talked like she hadn't in months, with her eyes shining bright. Her tiredness was gone and instead she felt excited. She didn't know what the future would be, but she knew what it wouldn't be. It wouldn't be long hours at a job she didn't care that much about, hours away from the people she loved the most. No, she'd figure out a way to stay home and still work at something she really cared about.

That night, for the first time since she had arrived, Althea felt that her time with the family was drawing to a close. It wouldn't be right away; there were still plenty of details to figure out. Like, for one, what exactly was Penny going to do? But Althea had faith- they'd figure it all out, and the family would be fine without her. When she was in her room that night, sitting quietly looking out the window, there was a knock at her door, and when she opened it there was Reinaldo (and Waffles, since you rarely saw one without the other) standing there with tears in his eyes. All she did was open her arms, and wrap him a loving hug, and he began to really cry.

"Oh Grandma, I don't want you to leave. I want you to stay here with us. I wish you wouldn't go. When you go away, I will be so lonely. I love you. Please don't..." but Althea shushed him before he could really ask her not to go. That just wasn't fair, and if he asked, she was afraid she wouldn't be able to leave. She hugged him and said, "It won't be for a while, so don't get upset now. We still have some time together, and I will be back sooner than 8 years, I promise you. I promise. I can't say when, but I promise it won't be so long next time, ok?"

Reinaldo nodded. He still couldn't speak, but he did think a cup of hot chocolate would make him feel better. How did he know Althea was thinking about leaving? It was the magical connection between them, and it would grow stronger as he grew up, if she had anything to do with it.

Down in the kitchen, the rest of the family sleeping, they sat in the warm yellow glow of the little lamp on the old wooden table, with their steaming mugs of hot chocolate. Althea looked at him seriously. He was only eight, but she had seen eight year olds do amazing things. There was one twelve year old boy she knew in the capitol city of Kathmandu who ran his family's tea shop and spoke four languages, all learned from travellers and tourists in the tea shop. Eight years old seemed so young, but she figured it was different from one boy to the next. And Reinaldo had always had a way of knowing things, which was why they were down in the kitchen instead of asleep in their beds.

They talked about Nepal, and Althea told him about Tenzin, the man he had seen in his dreams. "Oh Reinaldo, I think you two will be great pals. He can't speak much English, but he's learning. And even without much English, he makes me laugh so much. He thinks everything is so funny that I always end up laughing, too."

"But when am I going to meet him, Grandma? Is he going to come here? Do you think he'd like it here?"

Althea had a hard time imagining Tenzin on Millwood Lane. He didn't own any clothes that would look halfway normal to the people in the neighborhood. He didn't speak English, had never driven a car or flown in a plane or seen a computer or maybe even used a telephone. No, she had a better idea. Reinaldo would go with her to visit Tenzin for his summer vacation. But she didn't mention it to him. First she had to get Penny and Dan to say yes, and she figured that would not be easy.

The New Plan

That next week, Penny gave her notice at the bank. The people at the bank were really sorry to see her go. She did good work, and everybody liked her and she worked hard. They might have been a little bit jealous, too, since they were all going to stay there and work those long days while she figured out something fun to do. Then she started thinking about ways she could save money. Well, for one thing, she didn't have to spend money on clothes, since she wouldn't be dressing up every day. Maybe she would even get rid of her nice new car, that she paid for every month with a big payment, and get an older little car that cost less.

They were all at the breakfast table on Saturday, even Penny, who had told the bank she would stay until the first of the year, 6 weeks away, but would not be there for any more Saturdays no matter how busy they got. She would stay and train her replacement, a young woman with no children who didn't seem to mind the idea of long hours of work. Dan was reading the paper, and Tiffany was clearing the table after having helped make a great breakfast. She turned to her dad, "Are we going to go for a walk this morning? Because Becca wants me to go to the mall with her, and I have to let her know what time I can go?"

Althea cleared her throat. "If you don't mind, I would really like to talk to you both," looking at Penny and Dan, "before everybody starts off in their own directions for the day."

Dan smiled at Tiffany, "How about you and Becca go to the mall early, then we can walk late this afternoon, before it gets too cold. How would that be?"

She said that would work fine, she thought, she'd go call her friend, and left the room. Even though she and Becca would be spending most of the day together, they could be on the phone for the next hour, planning what they would wear to the mall, who they might see, and what they wanted to look for and buy.

Reinaldo took the hint right away, something he was really good at. "Uh, does anybody mind if Waffles and I go down to Wally's and watch cartoons?" Wally only lived about a block away, and his family, with five kids, always had cartoons on Saturday mornings, along with cereal and pillow fights and usually a big mess. Reinaldo loved it there, but he also loved coming home to the peace and quiet of his own home. Everybody nodded, so he ran upstairs to change out of his pajamas, grabbed his jacket and ran out the door, Waffles running along beside him as fast as his little legs would carry him.

When they were alone, with fresh cups of coffee in front of them, Althea told her plan. "I would like to take Reinaldo with me to Nepal for his summer vacation. I haven't said anything to him about it, of course, so we could talk about it first. If it's ok with you, I'll go back there in a month or two and get a nicer house than I had before, someplace he will feel more comfortable. Then, when school gets out, I'll come pick him up for a nice long visit. It is a long trip, so I would like to keep him there at least a month, and maybe two, before I bring him back. What do you think?"

There were so many questions. How would they know he would be safe? It was so far away, so strange. How did they know he wouldn't get hurt, or sick? Althea looked at them kindly. She knew their fears, but she also knew that she would do everything in her power to never let anything harm Reinaldo. And Tenzin would be a powerful protector, too. Not that there was anything bad that he needed protection from in her little village, but she wanted to take him traveling, show him the sights. It never hurts to have protectors, *especially* when they know magic.

An hour later, Tiffany came down the stairs dressed for the mall. Her eyelids shone with sparkling light, her lips gleamed with gloss, her hair stood up pretty much on its own, with the help of mousse and gel and spray. While her face looked like she was dressed for the prom, the rest of her looked like she was getting ready to take out the trash. Her jeans had holes, her shirt was wrinkled and pulled over a shiny tank top with sequins. Althea just grinned. She loved the crazy ways kids dressed, and she never ever told either Tiffany or Reinaldo to go change their clothes and put on something more becoming, or more "appropriate". No, Althea thought it was all great fun, watching what they would come up with next.

Dan and Penny and Althea were just cleaning up, anyway. It was decided, Reinaldo could go to Nepal with Althea for the 2 months next summer, provided Althea got a laptop and promised to keep in touch with them every day or two so they didn't worry too much. Provided Reinaldo got good grades this year (which he always did) and, most of all, provided he wanted to go. Penny and Dan themselves hadn't the slightest desire to go traipsing around in countries with uncomfortable bathrooms, if they had bathrooms at all, and hard beds, if they had them at all. In their hearts, they hoped Reinaldo would be more like them: he would tell his grandmother that he appreciated her offer, but that he would rather go to the YMCA day camp in town with the rest of his friends. That way, things would continue as they had for the last three summers, and Penny and Dan would know what Reinaldo was up to every day. As for Tiffany, the picture of her in a mud hut was beyond possibility. She would just never go for it.

But when Reinaldo came through the door a couple of hours later, his hair all wild from running home in the wind, his big eyes sparkling with excitement to share some crazy tale of Wally's house, Penny just sighed. She knew he was her son, but he looked so much like Althea! She could tug and press and comb and iron all she pleased; in the end, Reinaldo didn't care a hoot how he looked. He was after fun and magic. Penny shook her head. Tiffany you couldn't get away from a mirror, and Reinaldo never looked in one, unless it had to do with a magic trick.

And when they asked Reinaldo if he wanted to go with Althea to see where she lived for his summer vacation, he was so excited he could hardly stay in his skin. Jumping up and down, he said "Yes yes yes yes yes!!!!!!!" so excitedly that Dan finally told him, "Simmer down there pardner, before you get yourself one of those myocardial infarctions like I had!!" Then they all laughed, and Reinaldo hugged his parents hard, telling them, "Thank you so much for saying I could go!" that they just had to laugh again.

Sukoshi Rice

Christmas Vacation

The Christmas season that year was bittersweet, because everyone knew Althea would be leaving sometime in January, and Reinaldo was especially sad about that. There was also the madness of Penny's last few weeks at her job, and trying to get ready for Christmas. For the last few years, with Penny working so much and Dan being such a big potato, Christmas had taken on a pretty lackadaisical air. There was always a tree, but a small one, and Penny only got a few boxes of ornaments and lights out. This year, it was unanimous to get a huge big tree and totally decorate it with all the lights and ornaments they had, and to make a big celebration that Althea was with them and that Dan was healthy and that Penny would soon be home and not having to stress out at the bank all day long. Not to mention that Tiffany and Reinaldo didn't have school for a few weeks, but that happened every Christmas.

That Saturday they all went together to get a tree, in the morning, right after a breakfast of Althea's magical pancakes. Dan and Reinaldo put the tree in a bucket of water to soak before going into the stand while Penny and Althea went up in the attic to get the ornaments and lights. There were boxes of Christmas balls, some plain, some fancy, and a big box of lights, some tangled, some not. As Penny was carrying an armload downstairs, Althea spied an old trunk in the corner. It looked kind of familiar, like something you've seen in a dream and can't quite put your finger on. Quickly looking around to make sure she was alone, Althea went over to the trunk and blew some dust off the top. Under an inch or so of dust, these words were engraved:

**OPEN ONLY AT YOUR OWN RISK
AND FACE THE CONSEQUENCES**

Of course, she was instantly curious. Who had carved those words, and why? What could possibly be in an old trunk in Penny and Dan's attic? Even as she loved them dearly, Althea didn't kid herself. There wasn't a hint of magic, or trickery, or even bad thoughts around Penny and Dan. They were sweet kind normal people who never did anything alarming. Or really very fascinating, either. Hearing Penny on the stairs, Althea grabbed an old sheet and covered the trunk. She didn't know why, but some instinct told her that she should be the one to uncover its secrets.

Later that night, the Christmas tree was lit. Bubble lights bubbled, small white lights twinkled, and the star on the top of the tree glowed especially bright against the ceiling, just inches away. It was the biggest tree Reinaldo could remember ever having, and just looking at it made him feel great inside. No matter what you were thinking about, and even if your favorite person in the whole world was about to go half a world away, all those colored lights had to cheer you up. As the family sat around, they were quiet, each one lost in thoughts no one else could know. Tiffany thought about the new pink cell phone she wanted, Dan about the change in his family in the last few months since his heart "attack." Penny thought about what to get the kids for Christmas, while Reinaldo thought only about Althea. What was she thinking about? The trunk in the attic, and how, that night when everyone was asleep, she was going to investigate.

You know how when you want to stay up, everyone gets sleepy? The same thing seems to happen in reverse when you want everyone to go to sleep. Althea could hardly wait, but first, Tiffany remembered there was a paper she was supposed to write that she had totally forgotten about and the computer, remember?, was in Althea's room! Since Penny could type fast, she offered to type as Tiffany dictated, since it was already so late, but even with Penny helping, it took over an hour for the paper to be finished.

Reinaldo, had gone off to bed with Waffles, and Dan had gone to his bedroom to watch the late news, a habit Althea considered both unhealthy and unappealing. Why fill your head with bad news and bad pictures of bad people doing bad things just before going to sleep? She didn't get the feeling Dan would appreciate her point of view though, so she just let it go. In fact, tonight she thought it was a great idea for him to get in bed and watch TV.

Finally, it was silent in the big house, and Althea, flashlight in hand, picked her way up the old stairs to the attic, trying very hard not to make the boards creak, although that is almost impossible in an old house.

You know how creepy old attics can be? Althea didn't mind it at all. Normal every day creepy stuff never scared her. She was more bothered by things regular people thought were normal, like people living on fast food, and driving too fast and watching the bad news, and things like that. A creaky old attic was right up her alley.

Picking her way quietly around the empty boxes and cartons, she made her way back to the trunk with the white sheet over it. But where was it? She would have sworn it was right where she was standing, and with the white sheet over it, it would be a cinch to spot. But, where?...........oh, there it was, in the far corner. Odd and odder still, it seemed to have moved on its own. She gently pulled off the sheet and the trunk seemed to glow.

OPEN ONLY AT YOUR OWN RISK
AND FACE THE CONSEQUENCES.

Well, ok then. She was certainly up for an adventure, so slowly she pried the old trunk lid open. A light came from inside, and as she got the lid all the way open, Althea gasped. Inside the trunk was a vision of such loveliness it nearly took her breath away.

It was a summery day in a field, with huge green shade trees and a path that wandered along the edge of a small lake. The greens were so rich and green you could almost taste them, and the lake and the sky so blue it was like the very best summer day you have ever seen. In the distance of the field, Althea saw a human figure that looked so familiar. As he walked closer, she realized it looked like Tenzin, and her heart filled with happiness. So she leaned farther in, to get a better look when WHOOSH, she was pushed or pulled right into the trunk. For a second, all you could see was Althea's robes and skirts flying into the air, and then she was pulled down into the trunk and the lid slammed shut.

When Althea came to, she was lying under a big tree, and Tenzin was wiping her forehead with a cool cloth. The sun was shining bright, but there were no sounds, no birds singing, no wind through the trees. Tenzin didn't speak much English on a good day, but in this case, he didn't need it. He spoke to her without words, and at first, what he told her upset her greatly. "Don't travel with your grandson right now," he said. "Don't bring him here. The world is just too dangerous right now to bring an eight year old to Nepal. Too many people are fighting. It will get better someday, but right now is not the time for him to come."

Althea felt waves of sadness roll over her.

Tenzin didn't lose his sense of humor. He started to chuckle when he saw the look on her face, because he already knew she didn't have to be sad at all. "Don't worry," he whispered to her. "Soon I will be there with you. Trust me on this. Follow your heart."

And with that he hugged her and they passed the night under the sunlight trees in the middle of summer, without a care in the world.

When Althea woke up the next morning, she was in her little computer room, in the big comfy guest bed. She had slept late, much later than usual, and everyone was already up and in the kitchen when she arrived. "Grandma, are you ok? I was worried," Reinaldo grabbed her when she came in the doorway, looking flushed and befuddled and not at all her usual morning self.

"Well, yes, I think I'm ok, but I had the most curious dream, and I may not have slept enough, or maybe I slept too much....."

The whole family was looking at Althea by then, and Penny gently suggested her mom go back to bed for a while. "Go on, Mom. We got ourselves together, well sort of together, every morning when you weren't here, and we can manage today. Please go rest. You look a little done in."

When you're not used to strenuous magic, like a world in a trunk, it can be *very* tiring, so Althea kissed them all and went back to bed. Penny and Dan went off to work, and Reinaldo and Tiffany went to school. Tomorrow would be the first day of Christmas vacation, and then they would have every day to be together, until she went back to Nepal.

The thought made Althea gasp her breath. Nepal. She wasn't *going* back to Nepal. She remembered the trunk, and the "dream." Was it a dream? She remembered Tenzin, and how good it felt to be with him again, and felt so sad. And then she remembered his promise. He was coming here. Here? Millwood Lane?

The trunk! She would see if there were any more answers; even if it was exhausting to go into the other world, it was worth it to see Tenzin again.

Taking the steps two at a time, she raced up to the attic. In the corner stood a plain old trunk, covered with layers and layers of dust. Next to it, on the floor in a heap was an old white sheet, so full of dust that just moving it an inch could make you sneeze. It looked like nothing had been touched for *years*. When Althea finally got that dusty old trunk opened, it was full of the kids' school papers and old linens and photos from Dan's childhood and all kinds of old family stuff. Nowhere in it did Althea see any evidence of the wonderful sunlit meadow, and there was not a hint of Tenzin anywhere.

Now if this happened to you or me, we might think we were going crazy. For sure if we *told* most people about it, they would say, or at least think we were completely nuts. But Althea was used to magic, even if she was a bit rusty. It didn't surprise her, but it gave her some thinking to do.

"Follow your heart." Follow your heart. What does that mean to *do*? Althea went back downstairs, sat on her bed, wrapped herself in her big soft blue wool shawl, and closed her eyes. She waited, watching her breath. She tried not to think about anything, but just to listen. Suddenly she got an image in her mind, of the path on Overlook Mountain, and she had her answer. In order to know her heart, she would go out to the mountain and hike.

Quickly she packed lunch and a big bottle of water in her backpack, along with a silver survival blanket. She put on her warmest clothes, with long johns and hiking boots, a big parka and gloves and a wooly hat she brought from the mountains of Nepal. Driving Dan's old pickup truck, the one he used for chores around town, she took off for Overlook Mountain, excited to discover her heart's desire.

The last time she and Reinaldo and Tiffany had picnicked there, it had been late fall, with leaves still on the trees, chilly, but not cold. Today was cold, with an icy wind blowing through the bare trees. "This is interesting," she thought as she started up the path from the little parking lot at the base. "I wonder what is up here for me today!"

No surprise that Althea did not see another soul, or hear the sound of another voice. She hiked in silence through the snow, watching and waiting for a sign. And when she stopped to get her breath, she turned to look out over the valley and saw a sight that took her breath away.

Prayer flags! Tibetan prayer flags were flying in the valley. Where she thought she had imagined them in the fall, now she saw them clear as day, flapping in the wind, bright colors against the stark white background of snow. Without a second's hesitation, she started hiking toward them.

The path down toward the flags was slippery with snow, but it wasn't deep, and Althea walked as fast as she could, her heart racing with excitement. Surely here was the answer to Tenzin's mysterious message! Suddenly, she felt her feet slip out from under her on a patch of ice, and she fell down hard on the rocky path, her ankle twisting under her with a sharp shot of pain. She was only about 100 yards (one football field) from the clearing where the flags flew, but nearly a mile, back uphill to the path, then a twisting way down, to Dan's truck. She groaned with pain, and with a sudden picture of herself as a silly old woman. She had never thought of herself as old, or helpless, and she didn't like that picture one single bit.

Struggling to her feet, she began to hobble toward the flags when she heard a soft voice say, "Wait. Let me help you." Looking back up the path, she saw two men dressed in the dark burgundy robes of Tibetan lamas. There was a young man, about twenty or so, and an older man, about her age. It was the younger man who spoke to her. The older man just grinned and crinkled his eyes. Looking into his eyes, Althea felt peace come over her, and her whole body relaxed.

The monks searched until they found a good stout stick for her to lean on, then the younger one spoke again.

"Were you coming to the monastery?" he asked, his English a little hard to understand because of his accent.

When Althea answered in the Tibetan word for "Yes," their eyes lit up.

"Come," beckoned the young man. "We will make tea, then we will help you back to your truck."

Tea with the lamas was lovely, the same butter tea Althea had drunk with Tenzin in her little home in Nepal. The monastery was a simple place, built by hand of wood gathered from the forest and stones gathered from the mountain. It was small; only four monks lived there, but they were planning for more. As they talked, gesturing and laughing as Althea struggled in her basic Tibetan so that they could all join in, she felt so at home. Time flew by, and it was late afternoon when she looked out the window and realized the kids were home from school by now, and everyone would be worried sick if she didn't get back. Obviously the monastery didn't have a phone. It didn't even have electricity, much less a phone line.

The young monk saw the sudden distress on her face, and asked her what was wrong. When she explained her situation, that there was a family waiting for her, and that they would be worried, everyone became very grave. It was time to get her back to the truck.

While they had talked and laughed and visited, sharing their food, Althea's lunch, and cup after cup of the delicious tea, Althea had kept her ankle up, with snow packed around it. Now when she put it down to stand, the pain was intense. What to do? She tried to put her hiking boot on, but to jam it over the swollen ankle was more than she could bear. She was not going to be able to make it to the truck, much less drive it if she got there. To press the clutch pedal down took plenty of muscle on a good day. Right now, she knew she could not do it. There was only one thing she knew to do. She asked the monks if they would help her send a message to her grandson. If anyone could get it, Reinaldo could.

The monks stoked the fire to keep the room warm, and then they all sat down together on their meditation cushions. Althea told them a little bit about Reinaldo, especially what he looked like so that they could make a picture of him to send the message to. Then they talked about the message. Keeping it very simple, they decided to make a picture of the monastery, with Althea inside, and send him that. She added her own blessing and prayer, "I am ok. Don't worry. I'll be back as soon as I can."

With that they all sat down to concentrate and focus their energies on getting the message through to Reinaldo, so he could tell the family not to worry.

Meanwhile, back at Millwood Lane, Reinaldo, Tiffany and Penny were trying to figure out what was going on. Althea had *promised* to pick them up at school, being as it was the first minute of Christmas vacation, and take them out for ice cream or some other treat. When she wasn't there, they called Penny at the bank. Penny tried and tried to call the house, but nobody answered, so she left to go pick up the kids. It was not at all like Althea to forget to pick them up. It was so much not like Althea that even before they got home, Penny began to panic. Instead of going back to the bank, as *she* had promised, Penny called Dan at work.

"Hey sweetie," Dan answered when he heard Penny's voice. "What are you doing home at this time of day? Taking early retirement?"

Penny's voice was strained, "Dan, something happened to Mother. She promised the kids to pick them up, and the truck is gone and so is she. This can't be good. She would never forget to get them, and I have the worst feeling that she is not ok."

Dan's voice was soothing on the other end, "Take it easy Pen. Your mom is a grown woman and...." But Penny cut him off before he could say another word.

"I know Dan. I know she is a grown woman who traveled around the world and lived all kinds of strange places and was fine. But she is not fine now or she would have been at the school. The truck is gone, and we have to find her."

Dan begged her to be calm, and promised to come home as soon as he could.

Penny called Tiffany and Reinaldo into the kitchen, and as soon as they came in, they said, "Breathe, Mom. You have to breathe. Then you can relax and think straight."

It was too much for Penny, and she began to cry. Reinaldo asked her if she wanted some tea, and she nodded, miserably. Tiffany said she'd make it, 'cause Reinaldo felt funny and wanted to go to his room and be quiet for a little while. Penny told him to go ahead, if it made him feel better.

In his room, sitting on his bed with Waffles by his side, Reinaldo wrapped himself in his old black satin robe, worn and tattered now by countless magic tricks. He closed his eyes, and silently asked his grandmother to let him know she was all right. In a flash, he saw a homemade looking house built of logs and stone, with trees and a forest all around it, so that it was almost hidden by them. Althea sat inside the doorway, waving at him. He didn't know where she was, but inside himself he felt all warm and safe, so he knew she was fine.

Running back downstairs, Reinaldo told Penny and Tiffany what he had seen. Penny thought it was, well, cute, sort of, and she didn't doubt for an instant that the two could send each other messages without a phone or email, but it wasn't enough for her. She picked up the phone and called the police.

It was getting pretty dark when Althea and the monks heard people yelling. The young monk went outside and saw lights flashing up on the path, and heard people yelling "Althea, Althea, where are you??? Can you hear me??" Cupping his hands together to make a megaphone, he yelled out, "She is down here, she is safe."

With their big flashlights lighting the way, down the path came Dan and two sheriff's deputies. They carried some rescue gear, because when they found the truck at the entrance to the path up Overlook, they knew she was up there somewhere, and feared she had been hurt and couldn't make it back down. What they didn't realize was what a good time she had been having with her new friends, who were very sorry to see her go and made her promise to come back as soon as her ankle was healed.

With a makeshift stretcher held between them, the cops and Dan took turns carrying Althea back to the road. It was long hard work, and Dan thanked his stars over and over for having gotten into better shape in the last few months. In fact, he was in better shape than the cops, and his real worry was that one of them was going to have to be carried!

When Althea hobbled through the door, Penny burst into tears again. Even though Dan had called her from the car, she had been so worried that the relief made her cry. Althea was in pain, but not too much to hug her daughter, and say, "It's ok, don't worry. It's just my ankle and I'll be fine." Tiffany just grinned, but Reinaldo piped up, "I knew you were ok, Grandma. I saw you!" Althea just gave him a grin, and then announced that a hot bath and an ice bag for her ankle were just what she needed, and everyone took off to get that together, and to make her as comfortable as she could be.

Life on Millwood Lane was not what they had been planning for Christmas vacation Even though Althea's ankle was badly sprained, and not broken, it was swollen and painful for several days. Ice skating was out of the question, along with long walks, short walks, shopping ("Yay!" she thought, "No malls!") or anything else that required much time on her feet. For the first time since she arrived, Althea got taken care of, instead of taking care of everyone. Since Penny and Dan still had to go to work, she sat in the kitchen with her leg propped up and directed Tiffany and Reinaldo in making wonderful gingerbread cookies, and brownies, and yummy dinners they all ate together at night. In that warm Christmas kitchen, with delicious smells coming from the oven, Reinaldo turned to Althea on the second or third afternoon with a sad face.

"What in the world is the matter?" Althea asked him. "Your face is so sad it hurts my heart."

"I can't stand for you to go away again," Reinaldo muttered, head down so no one would see the tears welling up and spilling over from his eyes.

"Oh my goodness!" Althea exclaimed. "I've been so busy with all this mess with my ankle and trying to get around that I completely forgot to tell you my news. I'm not going back to Nepal. I'm staying right around here!"

Reinaldo and Tiffany both stopped right in their tracks, one with the mixer in the air, the other greasing a cookie sheet. They looked like they had been zapped.

And right then, Althea told them the whole story. Well, almost the whole story. She left out the part about the trunk, since she didn't think it was anybody's business that she spent the night in the attic in a trunk with Tenzin. She just told them he had come to her in a dream, and told her he was coming.

Tiffany had a look on her face that- well, it was quite a look for her. She thought she was pretty sophisticated and all, but her grandmother with a boyfriend! And a Tibetan one, at that, who hardly spoke English? No, it was the grandmother with a boyfriend at all that jammed her gears.

Reinaldo felt happier than he had ever been in his life. Even though his trip to Nepal was postponed, maybe forever, he didn't care. That trip was only because his grandmother would be living there, and he didn't want her to go. Knowing that she, and Tenzin, would be close by, he grinned until he felt silly, like his face was going to break.

Christmas Morning

Who doesn't like Christmas morning? If you celebrate Christmas in your family, you must know what it's like to lie in bed in the dark, trying to stay in bed long enough not to be ridiculous (you can't get your stocking before 5 a.m. in some families, and sometimes even later.) Reinaldo was usually like that. After all, he was only eight years old, and it is hard to sleep on Christmas morning at that age, but when he woke up at 5 or 6, he started grinning. He remembered that Althea wasn't leaving, and that was the best present of all. Snuggling Waffles up next to him, their two heads on the pillow, he fell back asleep.

Pancakes, coffee, hot chocolate, cinnamon, maple syrup and butter- the smells were almost as delicious as the food by the time everyone came into the kitchen. Althea was directing Penny and Dan, who were cooking up a storm. While the kids got their stockings and brought them into the kitchen to unpack them, the grownups set the table and sat down with their coffee. Reinaldo could hardly stop grinning. He was just so happy, that everything was so good. His dad was well, his mom would be home soon, his grandma was staying, his sister, well, she was about the same but at least she was nicer since she walked with Dan every day. Nah, even Tiffany was ok, he had to admit.

After breakfast it was time for presents. There were toys and books and sweaters and CD's and a new huge flat screen TV from Dan to the whole family. Althea had made Tiffany the funkiest dress of lace and spandex and velvet, and Tiffany just *loved* it. It would be perfect to wear to Anita's party on Friday, with her big black boots and Althea's silver scarf ("Oh, do you mind if I borrow it?" Tiffany would innocently ask on Friday night as she was running out the door.) For Reinaldo, there was a meditation cushion and a dark blue shawl made of the softest and warmest wool from Nepal. As soon as he sat on his cushion, Reinaldo felt right at home, and the shawl wrapped around him like a cloud, the warmest and safest thing. Of course he wouldn't take the shawl out of the house: he knew the very best place for it was folded neatly in his room on top of the cushion. That way, every time he wanted a quiet time, he knew just where to go.

It was late in the morning, nearly noon, when Althea said she would like to take some cookies and a cake up to the monks on Overlook Mountain. Even though they didn't celebrate Christmas, they knew about it, of course, and she wanted to bring them some Christmas cheer and also thank them for their wonderful hospitality the day she fell.

Penny and Dan were concerned for her. Could she make the walk? Why didn't she wait? But she just gave them her sympathic look and said, "I know you two are worried, but my ankle is quite all right now for such a short walk. It's been warm enough to have melted the iciness, and besides, I was hoping Reinaldo would go with me and meet the monks and keep me company."

What could they say? Reinaldo looked like he would burst if they didn't say yes. It *was* a beautiful sunny day. Tiffany was off to her friend Anita's house to spend a couple of hours comparing new clothes and makeup, and then they would probably go to a movie with Becca, if her family said it was ok. Dan and Penny could have the whole house to themselves for the afternoon.

"Take my car," Dan said, smiling. "The front wheel drive will be the best if you hit any bad patches on the road, and you won't have to fight that old truck clutch."

Althea and Reinaldo went into the kitchen and began to pack Christmas treats. They had made so many cookies and gingerbread men and muffins and cupcakes when Althea's ankle had to be up that they had plenty to choose from.

Let's see, a plastic container full of oatmeal raisin cookies, and another one of big fat chocolate chips. A small one of those fudgy yummy brownies that would make you sick if you ate too many. A box of gingerbread men with those little candy pearls for eyes, some plain old shortbread cookies that just melted in your mouth, and a tin of cupcakes with all kinds of frosting. By the time they had them all packed up, it was time to go. With their boots and parkas and mittens and hats, Althea and Reinaldo looked like they were going on an Arctic expedition.

Althea had learned from last time, better to be warm and have things you need with you.

Overlook Mountain looked beautiful in the sunshine, with the snow glinting and throwing off sparks of color in the light. They walked quickly to the path to the little monastery, and as they turned down it, they saw the prayer flags flying. "How could I have thought I imagined them?" Althea wondered. They were clear as day, bright colors against the white snow.

As they neared the building, the door opened and the young monk who had saved Althea, the one who spoke English, stepped out. With a big smile, and a big bow, he welcomed them, bowing again to Althea and taking Reinaldo's hand to shake. In their turn, Althea and Reinaldo held out their boxes of goodies and said, "Merry Christmas."

"Yes," the young monk replied, a big smile on his face, "It is a very good Christmas for us. We have had wonderful news from home. But first, please come in, and we will make tea."

Reinaldo's eyes widened at the inside of the monastery's main hall. Althea had felt so at home she hadn't really noticed much, but to Reinaldo, it was new and exotic and very exciting. The room was made all of wood, with a bench built into the wall all the way around. In the center of the room there was a fireplace of sorts, really just a sunken pit in the floor that went down to the earth below, and that's where the fire burned. It was kind of smoky standing up, but when you sat down, it was fine. There were multi-colored cushions placed all around the fire pit on the floor, so you could actually sit close to the fire and stay very warm that way. A big iron teakettle hung on an iron hook over the fire, and the monk swung it over to him to add more water before swinging it back over the fire. Cooking with fire! Reinaldo had only done that a couple of times on camping trips. That was really fun in itself, but here there was so much more.

At the far end of the room, sitting up on a kind of a throne, was a large statue of the Buddha. Reinaldo knew a little about Buddha, from Althea's stories and from school, where they had studied a little about different religions. But this Buddha was BIG. Reinaldo started to wonder, "how in the world did these monks get such a huge statue here?" But no sooner had that thought crossed his mind when Althea gave an exclamation that sounded like "WHOOSH." He didn't realize she could speak their language (she really couldn't very much, but she did know some words. She had just said "WOW!" in Tibetan.)

The young monk was sitting very quietly with a very excited Althea, and Reinaldo wanted to know what was going on. She explained, "This brother has just told me their good news. It seems there are three men coming from their home in Tibet. They are not monks, they are refugees. They are coming to help build a larger monastery, because they are expecting nearly thirty monks to come here to live in the next few years. I think maybe that was Tenzin's message. Maybe he is one of the three men."

Even though that seemed like kind of a long shot to Reinaldo, he didn't say so. His grandmother looked so happy, and he figured she knew more about this business anyway. And, since believing it made her so happy, he wanted it to be true.

Christmas tea was a delicious treat for the monks. Mostly they lived on tea and bread and whatever vegetables they cooked. None of the four was exactly a gourmet chef, although they did okay. Reinaldo liked his buttered tea, especially with cookies, which the monks insisted they share. Althea looked thoughtful the whole time, not speaking much, just watching, happy to see that Reinaldo was so comfortable and having fun with the monks.

Too soon it was time to leave. Althea seemed regretful to go, and Reinaldo could feel it, even though he didn't want to get stuck on the mountain in the dark. Remembering her last adventure, Althea agreed with him that they needed to get a move on before it started getting dark. In the winter, late afternoon turns quickly to night, and she was taking no chances with Reinaldo.

As they got in the car and headed down hill, Althea spoke her question slowly and thoughtfully, as if she were just figuring it out as she said it. "Reinaldo, what would you think of my moving part time to the monastery, and living part time with you? I'm sure they wouldn't mind my building a room on, and they could sure use a good cook! I love being with you, but I love being there, too. I am used to that kind of living, with no TV or phone to distract me, and I didn't realize how much I missed it."

Reinaldo looked at her thoughtfully. "Well, you *were* going to be in Nepal by now, or pretty soon, so I think it's a whole lot better if you are at the monastery right over the mountain. Do you think I could come stay with you there sometimes? I liked it there, too, and I would like to learn to speak their language."

Althea could only smile at him. She was so happy right then, she got those happy tears in her eyes she had to wipe away to keep driving. In silence, they drove the rest of the way home, both with happy thoughts of the future dancing in their heads.

Sukoshi Rice

Christmas Vacation Ends

By the time they got home, dark had pretty well set in, and they walked into a scene of chaos. Penny was just getting to the point where she was starting to pace the floor, and as soon as they walked into the kitchen she whirled around angrily at her mother, "I have been worried sick. Last time you went up the mountain, remember what happened?! And this time you had Reinaldo! I was just sick, and I wish you thought about my feelings more."

Penny looked about to cry, and Althea put her hand on Penny's arm. "I am so sorry. It's not snowing out and it just now got dark. I didn't know you would worry, and I'm so sorry you did."

Reinaldo just put his arms around his mom, and hugged her as tight as he could. "I'm sorry, mom," he whispered. "But we really had fun. Will you go with us some time?" He was so excited, with his face so bright and flushed, that Penny had to laugh.

"I'm a goon!" she exclaimed with a big sigh. "I worry about so many things. It's a wonder the sun rises and sets without *my* help."

Althea just hugged her then, and asked if she wanted help with dinner, which she did. (Who refuses that???)

Tiffany and Dan came in from their walk around the neighborhood just as Reinaldo was setting the table, then they all sat down to eat. It was great to all be together, thought Reinaldo, watching his mom and dad laughing and talking. It was so different from before, before Althea came, before Penny decided to leave the bank. It was so much better now because everyone was so much happier.

Althea brought up her idea after a while. "Hey everyone, I've already talked this over a little with Reinaldo on our way home, oh, Tiffany, in case you didn't know, Reinaldo and I went up to the little monastery on Overlook this afternoon to take some cookies to the monks. I had this idea I wanted to run by you all before I asked them. I like it up there with them. There is no electricity and no phone, so no TV or computer or any of that. Life is very simple there, pretty much like my home in Nepal was. I was wondering if they would let me build a room or a little cottage for myself so I could spend time up there with them. I could use the peace and quiet for meditation time, and they could sure use a cook. I think I could really be a help for them."

The whole family went really quiet, then Reinaldo piped up, "It was so neat there. Those guys are really nice, and we could go visit sometimes, too!" Once again, his enthusiasm saved the day, and everyone laughed. Penny reached over and patted her mother's hand, "I want you to do whatever you want to do, mom. But do you think you could just stay here for a few weeks until I quit at the bank and maybe get my feet on the ground about what I am going to do next?"

Althea nodded, then she added, "I'm not talking about forever, all the time. I'd like to go back and forth, so I could always be here if you need me. We couldn't build anything up there until springtime anyway and besides, I'm not planning to go very far away again."

When he heard that, Reinaldo grinned until his face hurt. He thought he couldn't be happier.

It never lasts long enough, does it? Just when you get used to sleeping late and eating lots of cookies and good stuff like that, it's time to go back to school. Reinaldo was kind of dreading it, because he liked hanging out at home with Althea, going to visit the monks (although they had only had one more short visit, and then a big snow came.) Tiffany loved school, especially right after getting a bunch of new clothes to show off, but even during vacation, she was off with her friends more than she was home. Penny was still at the bank, but in her last week of it, and it was starting to stress her out pretty badly. Her replacement wasn't learning as fast as Penny had hoped, so she was staying late with her, going over and over everything, trying to make sure that when she left, things ran smoothly. One night she got home after nine. It was just like the old days, and she was so tired she started to cry.

"I don't know what we would have done without you, Mom," she sniffled to Althea. "You have really kept us together the whole time you've been here, and I am so glad you could and I feel pretty guilty about it, too."

But Althea just gave her a look that shushed her. "That's what I'm here for, and I'll stay until you don't need me so much, so don't worry. I like it here. I've been very happy with you all, so don't start thinking you asked me to do too much. You didn't have to ask. I'm your mother, and I love you all, and that's that!"

Penny quit crying then, and gave her mom a weepy looking grin. "I can hardly wait to be home every day, even though I have no idea what I am going to do for work and that is really scaring me. Do you have any ideas for me?"

Althea hugged Penny. "It's late, you have to be at the bank again at eight in the morning. Instead of talking about this now, let's wait until the week is out, when we can really sit down and get into it, ok? I don't usually find I am the most imaginative when I am tired, do you?"

So Penny trundled off to a bath and bed, and everyone else went to bed. Althea sat on her meditation cushion, with her blue shawl like a cloud of sky wrapped around her, and drifted off to Nepal, to visit with Tenzin, to see the blue sky and hear the bells on the goats as they trotted by her little house, early in the morning.

The last weekend of the vacation, the last weekend of freedom from the daily schedule of school, was Penny's first weekend of freedom. While Reinaldo had a long face, and Tiffany endlessly planned what to wear with what, Penny felt like she had just taken off a huge and heavy backpack. She couldn't believe it, she was finished with that job, and she celebrated by sleeping and sleeping and sleeping.

The kids couldn't believe their mom could sleep nearly around the clock, but Dan and Althea took them out for pizza, and to the movies, and anything they could think of to let Penny sleep. It was her way of healing, of letting go of all that stress, and her body needed the relief. On Monday morning, Dan took the kids to school, and Penny and Althea sat in the kitchen, drinking coffee from big colorful mugs, relaxing in the quiet.

"I've been thinking," Althea started. "It would be no good to think of something to do that you don't love, because you already did that at the bank. You were very good at what you did, but it didn't make you feel good. It took energy from you. Let's make a list of the things you love to do the most, ok?"

Penny thought that was a great idea, only her first thing she loved to do the most was sleep. Althea thought that was probably just temporary, and since she'd never heard of anyone being paid to sleep, she hoped so. "No, think of something else, or do you want to wait and do this later?"

"You know what I love, Mom? I love to read, and I love to walk in the woods and be quiet, and I love to cook, believe it or not. When I had time, I was pretty good. All the things I can think of right now are like that, quiet things because I think I just need to rest. I really can't get revved up yet, until I feel strong again. I just didn't realize how tired I've been, and how that job drained me."

"In that case," Althea smiled "I think we should dedicate today to be a rest and rejuvenation day, and spend as much time doing the things you like as we can. I would love a nice long meditation, and a nice long stretching session, with a hot bath and maybe baking some more cookies thrown it."

Penny gave her mom a big grin. "I have a better idea. Let's celebrate with a spa day, my treat. I got a bunch of money when I left the bank, and I could use a day of being treated like a Queen. And so could you, after all you've done for us!"

Althea started to protest, but it was no use. Penny was so excited about sharing with her mom, there was no way to say no. And besides, what kind of person turns down a day at the spa??? Even when you are used to peace and quiet and meditation and stretching, having someone rub your back with hot stones in a dark quiet room with candles flickering and soft music playing? It was a no brainer!

It was a Monday morning, the spa was open, and in the middle of winter, happy to have the business, any business. But when they got there, the spa owner looked grim faced. "Uh-oh" they both thought, "this is no way to start a relaxing experience." She looked up at them, and then gave a tired smile. "I am happy to see you both. I am just a little put out because our receptionist quit, but your therapists are here, and happy to take care of you."

A young woman named Ariel came out from a back room and took Penny into the room where she got a facial. She felt all the tension in her face, from all that smiling and all those years of makeup at the bank, rinsing off her skin. From there, a woman named Diane took her to a different room for her massage, where she lay quietly while all her tensions and anxieties were kneaded out of muscles she didn't even know were sore. Through it all, Penny and her therapists barely spoke so she could soak in the silence and rejuvenate.

Althea didn't need rejuvenation since she stayed pretty relaxed, but she was all for silence and rest. While Penny got her facial, Diane massaged Althea first. Diane had just had a big mug of coffee and she was wound up like a top! Althea got an earful, in a very non-professional but very entertaining way, about the runaway receptionist. It seems she was just too young (according to Diane) and having boyfriend troubles with some guy who wasn't worth the effort (according to Diane) and had just picked up and gone off with him and left the spa in a lurch.

"Hmmm," thought Althea, "I hope that's the end of the story" as she settled in to the warmth of the hot rocks gliding up and down her back, relaxing her more than she had been in a long time. Two hours later, Penny and Althea met up in the spa lobby, glowing and feeling great.

"How about lunch, Mom? Wanna go to Edgar's?" Edgar's was a really popular restaurant in town with local people, full of good food and warmth, not much on frills and amenities. All the waitresses wore whatever they wanted and most of them knew everyone who came in. It was a really friendly place.

In the car, and over lunch, Penny couldn't stop talking about how much she loved being at the spa, how restful and quiet it was, how great her treatments were, and how much she loved being there (did she already say that?) Finally, Penny, still pink and glowing from her treatments, blurted out "I think I'll help that poor woman out and be her receptionist a couple of hours a day. It would be something to do while I figure out what I really want to do, and it did sort of just land with a thump at my feet."

Althea looked carefully at Penny and said, "Why don't you give yourself time to think this one through, Pen? We'll get Reinaldo and go home and take naps, then we can talk it over at dinner tonight."

And that's what they did, Penny sleeping the rest of the afternoon away while Althea and Reinaldo snuggled on the couch, reading, and even doing homework. As long as Althea was there to talk to, the TV did not go on until Dan or Penny turned it on for the evening news. Even Tiffany was careful about that, and besides, she couldn't see her face too well in the TV screen, so she was more interested in the big mirror in her room, looking for nasty stuff some days, and how perfect she looked on good days.

That night, at dinner, Penny and Althea told the family about their day, about the spa and the runaway receptionist with the worthless boyfriend (according to Diane.) Then Penny brought up what she had thought, that she might help out by being receptionist there a couple of mornings a week, just to try it out. They just stared at her.

"You have *so* got to be kidding me, babe," exploded Dan. "You would trade in a good job at the bank with lots of stress and lots of money to be a receptionist in a *spa* for a lot of stress and much less money? Are you really thinking of that?"

Tiffany even chimed in, "Mom, you know most of those women who go to spas are rich and snobby and they complain about *everything* and they *always* complain at the receptionist! *Always.* You would be *bombarded.*"

Althea kept quiet, then volunteered, "It was really wonderful getting treatments there. I'm not sure it would be so wonderful on the other side of things, just like eating a great meal in a restaurant doesn't mean it's peaceful in the kitchen. But as an experience, it might be a good one to have. Most of them are."

Dan stared at her, covering Penny's hand with his big warm one, "Hon, we have plenty of money for now. *Please* give yourself a week without working or thinking about working. You are so responsible and this is another thing that could start out small and simple and end up taking you away from us again. I can't support that."

Penny looked at him, at all of them and sighed. "I know, "she said. "I better learn to relax first, and then figure out a fun, relaxed way to earn some money. If there is one. You think there is one?" she asked, looking at Dan. "You think I can find something I can do and stay even borderline calm and not get all wound up and nuts?"

Althea cleared her throat in that way people do when they have something to say. "Honey, if you meditated every day, you sure would stay calmer. I learned that, and I could teach you what I know. Reinaldo knows how If nothing else it calms you down."

Penny smiled, "You're all right. Yes, Mom, I would like to try meditating and see if I would get calmer. And Dan, you're right. I don't need another taking-care-of-everybody-in-the-place kind of job. And Tiffany, I don't know if all the women who come in the spa are rich or not, but I do know that if they want to complain with all the wonderfulness that goes on in there, I sure don't want to hear about it! So, that's settled! From now on I will just make sure I earn enough money to go to the spa *and* have the time to do it!"

They all laughed. Penny was back on the team.

Cookies

The next morning, by the time Althea got home from taking the kids to school, Penny was already in the kitchen, mixing up a giant batch of chocolate chip cookies. "Y'know what I want to do, Mom? I want to take a really pretty little bag of cookies to all those people I worked with at the bank. They will just love it and it will give me a chance to visit. I'll make these chocolate chips, and then some oatmeal raisins, and maybe I dunno a fruit bar or something?"

Althea jumped right in. "We have got the *best* recipe around here for those apricot bars. How much you got in that mixer? I'd like to take cookies to those poor monks while you go to the bank. I bet they haven't had a cookie since the last time I was there, weeks ago."

For the next couple of hours, they mixed and measured, laughed and talked, until the counter was piled high with cookies and apricot bars. Then it was white paper and ribbon until they had eighteen pretty packages for the bank, a big bag for the monks, and plenty left over for Dan and the kids when they got home.

Penny put on a nice pair of pants and a sweater. This was her first visit to the bank as a retired person and she was kind of nervous. Then she laughed. She had only really retired four days ago!

Althea got on her hiking boots and parka and got an emergency blanket and a bottle of water. "I'm taking Waffles," she suddenly decided. "In case something happens to me again, he'll know what to do."

Penny just looked at her. Like *what* would Waffles know to do besides lick her and bark and eat the cookies? But she kept that to herself.

Penny had a great time at the bank, visiting with her friends, who used to be her co-workers. When Cheryl Peterson, who used to work late with her, took her bag of cookies, she gave Penny a big hug. "This is the sweetest thing for you to do, Penny. You are so thoughtful. You deserve something really wonderful to happen for you."

"Thank you, Cheryl," Penny said thoughtfully. "I really wonder what I'm going to do next, but since I'm not busy with anything yet, I thought you all might like cookies."

She went from person to person giving her little bags, but Linda Reynes and Rajit Rao, Urmi's dad, were away for the day, which left Penny with two bags extra.

She still had some time before getting Reinaldo at school, so she thought, "Why not? I'll take them to the spa to that poor spa owner and my nice treatment girls."

When she walked in the door, the spa owner was not there. In the receptionist seat sat a new young girl (too young, Diane the massage therapist might say) studying her nails and looking bored.

"Hello, how may I help you?" she said, looking up. She had blonde hair, and way too much makeup (according to Penny this time) but she was friendly enough.

"Is Irene in?" asked Penny, remembering the owner's name.

"Who may I tell her is here?" the girl asked, more careful and polite now.

"Just tell her it's a friend, with cookies," was Penny's answer.

When Irene came out, Penny gave her the two bags of cookies, saying, "You might not even remember me, but I had such a wonderful day here, so I brought some cookies for you and the young ladies who work here as thanks."

By the time Penny and Reinaldo and Tiffany got home, the phone was already ringing. People wanted more of those cookies. Dave Reinhardt, Cheryl Peterson's boss, was having a party at his house for his old college friends that weekend, and his wife wanted to know if they could buy three dozen cookies. "Sure!" said Penny, writing it down.

Anne Gregory called. Her daughter's birthday was next week. Of course they were having a cake, but she would also like to serve those delicious apricot bars, if Penny was making them to sell. She thought maybe two dozen, or maybe three, and did she make any other fruit bars? Penny said, "Sure! "and wrote it down.

The spa owner, Irene, called. "Wow!" she said. "You make fantastic cookies. I'd like to sell them here, in little bags like you had them. Can we start with maybe three dozen bags?"

"Sure," said Penny, writing it down.

By the time Tiffany and Reinaldo came back into the kitchen from changing out of their school clothes, Penny was sitting at the table with a glazed look in her eyes.

"Mom, what is it?" asked Tiffany, with a worried look. She shook her mom's arm to get her attention.

"Kids," Penny said, standing up and stretching, "I think I just went into the cookie business."

They all grinned. What a great business to be in!

Well, it *seemed* like a great business. I mean, everything smelled great, and tasted even better. The house smelled wonderful. But how were they going to earn money with cookies? How much did a cookie cost to make? How much should they sell them for?

Penny, Tiffany and Reinaldo piled back in the car and headed for the supermarket. They bought butter, flour (organic and plain, whole wheat and white), sugar (organic and plain, brown and white), oatmeal, raisins (organic and plain), dried apricots, vanilla and cinnamon. And then they went home.

By the time Dan and Althea both got home, Dan looking kind of tired from a long day, Althea glowing from a day on the mountain with the monks, Penny was cooking dinner and Tiffany and Reinaldo were sitting at the kitchen table surrounded by cookie ingredients, putting numbers into their calculators and trying to figure out how much a cookie cost to make.

"What is going on here?" asked Dan. "Are we opening a bakery?"

"No," grinned Reinaldo. "It's better than that, Dad. We're opening a cookie factory. Everybody in town wants Mom and Grandma's cookies! Everybody!"

Althea gave Penny a funny smile. "Is that true, Honey? Did you get some orders for cookies?"

Tiffany, who usually was too cool to get into family discussions, just about exploded! "Tell 'em, Mom! Tell 'em how many cookies have been ordered!"

Penny grinned. "Right now we have 17 dozen chocolate chips, 12 dozen oatmeal raisin, and about 14 dozen bars and brownies and other cookies. Altogether we have 33 dozen, give or take a little.

We bought all this stuff to figure out how much a cookie costs. Tell you the truth, I didn't expect THIS!"

So over dinner they talked it all over. Organic was definitely more expensive, but it was what they had always used, at least since Althea came back and did the shopping, and that was part of why people loved their cookies. They just tasted better. Then again, you didn't eat cookies to be healthy, exactly, so it might be ok to do ½ organic, ½ plain. Everybody agreed. Who would buy a $3.00 cookie? They had to be practical.

After dinner they all sat at the table. If 24 cookies used 3 cups of flour, how many cookies would be in a pound! Yikes. The cookbooks had "conversion tables" where cups were changed to ounces and pounds, so with everybody working, and Penny really glad she had worked at the bank so her math was top notch, cookie prices started to get real.

Whoops. They had forgotten gas to heat the oven.

And gas for the car to deliver the cookies.

Whoops, they had forgotten to pay themselves.

By the time they came up with some prices, Reinaldo and Waffles were curled up on the couch, fast asleep. That was just too much math for one night. Tiffany was really proud she had been able to figure so much out, and when Dan said to her "Tiff, you really know your math. I'm impressed!" she glowed like a light.

They needed cookie bags and cookie boxes. Most of all they needed a name.

What were they going to call their cookies?
Hugging each other good night, Dan carried Reinaldo up to bed while everyone else said, "Let's sleep on it and in our dreams we'll find the name."

In the morning, Dan took the kids to school so Penny and Althea could mix and bake. All day long, until it was time to go to the school, they baked cookies. It was fun, and they talked and played music and drank coffee. And all day long they took more cookie orders.

"Let's get out of here for a bit," said Penny. "Let's pick up the kids and go to Edgar's and have something to eat and just get away from cookies for a minute so we can think!"

Althea laughed. She loved baking cookies, even hundreds of them, and thought the most fun business had come to Penny. They'd figure it out.

But when they got to Edgar's, they had no sooner sat down than Edgar himself came over to their booth.

"Hey Penny, hey Althea, hey kids. I hear you're making some pretty awesome cookies. I've been hearing from everyone who comes in that I should buy your cookies to sell here. Thing is, I can't, but I'd like to. For me to sell your cookies, they have to be baked in a kitchen that is approved and inspected by the Health Department. You get one of those, and put me on your list for about 20 dozen a week, easy."

Penny and Althea looked at each other. They didn't even have a name for their cookies yet, they hadn't even gotten there, but they knew they needed a big approved cookie factory for their cookie business, because it was already outgrowing their kitchen.

Reinaldo smiled shyly. "Do you think we could call them Penny & Althea's Magic Cookies? You know, with the "and" sign instead of the word, and maybe a rainbow and some stars on the label?"

Althea said, "Well, I don't know. It's your mom's cookie business, not mine."

"Nonsense!" Penny retorted. "If it wasn't for you, I wouldn't know how to make cookies. I want to do this with you, Mom, if you want to?"

"Penny & Althea's Magic Cookies" were born. And nobody but Althea and Reinaldo knew those cookies were really magic, because every time Althea made some, she prayed for the people who ate them to be healthy and happy. She prayed health and happiness right into the cookies, so when people ate them, they felt so good they wanted more!

Penny found out soon enough what the magic ingredient was.

The next day, while they were finishing up the orders of cookies for the weekend, Penny happened to look up and see Althea holding her hands over a bowl of cookie dough with her eyes closed. "Hey Mom, what were you just doing?" she asked when Althea opened her eyes.

"I was praying. I was praying that wherever these cookies go, they bring happiness and good health to the person eating them. I always pray when I cook. You didn't know that?"

Penny felt so stupid. "No, I guess I've been too out of it or something to notice! You wanna teach me the prayer?"

"No, Sweetie," said Althea. "There isn't <u>A Prayer</u>. You just pray from your heart for the health and happiness of the people who eat the cookies. That's all. And that love goes into the cookies, and it works. You've seen how it works. All these people eating the cookies feel GOOD when they eat them, so they want more."

"You mean the secret ingredient is love? That's it?" Penny asked. She looked kind of stunned, like she thought it was going to be some special maple sugar or exotic dried fruit.

Love. What a great secret ingredient. They would put it on the label, that each cookie was made of flour, sugar, eggs, butter, flavorings and love.

Just then the phone rang. It was Nancy Gibson, an old friend of Penny's from the bank who had quit years before to have a baby.

"Hey Pen," she said in her cheerful voice, "I hear you've got quite a cookie operation going on. I was just wondering if you need some help with baking. Now that Miranda's started school, I've got time from 9-3 every day, and I *love* to bake cookies. Want some help?"

"Sure!" said Penny. She liked Nancy, who was a happy, positive person and a real hard worker. "The only thing is, we're already a little cramped here at the house. But we've actually been talking about getting a place just for cookies, with a Health Department approved kitchen so we can sell them to stores and restaurants, too."

"You have?" Nancy sounded excited. "Did you know Irving Glassman wants to sell his bakery? The old one on the edge of town, out by the school? He said he and Miriam are just getting too old to run it, even with help, and they want to sell it and move to Florida and play golf and lie in the sun. Why don't you talk to him?"

So, cookies done and cooling, Althea and Penny climbed in the car to stop by Glassman's bakery before getting the kids at school. On the way, Penny looked over at her mom. "By the way, Mom. I totally forgot to ask with all the cookie stuff going on, but how was your visit to the monks? What's going on with them?"

Althea grinned. "They said the men coming to help them will be here in a couple of weeks, so they are really happy because with how hard they have to work in winter, they could sure use a hand. They do ok with food and all, but I know they loved those cookies. I've been meaning to get back up there, maybe take a bag of groceries because they do the whole thing on foot, but I've been too busy baking cookies to even think about it. Maybe Sunday afternoon, if the weather behaves, Reinaldo and I will go, if that's ok with you."

"Sure," said Penny. These days she was so happy, she said "sure" to just about everything.

Glassman's Becomes Magic

Inside Mr. Glassman's bakery, it was quiet and still. "Hello? Hello back there." Althea called. "Hello Mr. Glassman, are you back there?"

Through a curtain that divided the little showroom part, with its bread racks and cases of bagels and scones from the bakery in the back, came Irving Glassman. His hair looked snow white from flour, but it really almost was, anyway. He wore a huge apron, covered with flour, and he even had a light dusting in his eyebrows. He looked kind of like a snowman!

"Hello, Ladies," he said with a smile. "What would you like today? A little rye bread? Some nice hot cheese scones?"

"Well," said Penny, very politely, "those sound very good, and we probably will get some, but really we came because we heard you and your wife would like to move somewhere warm, and if you would like to sell the bakery, we are looking for a place to bake our cookies. We are looking for a bakery."

"Sell the bakery??? I couldn't sell the bakery!" Mr. Glassman exclaimed. "I built this bakery business from nothing! I couldn't let it go."

He studied their faces. Penny looked like she might cry, she had been so excited. Then he smiled. "I couldn't let it go to just *anybody*, but somebody who really loved baking, and who could pay enough to send us on our way, well, that I might consider." And he gave them such a wink, flour fell from his eyelashes and made them laugh. Penny's face went from sad to so happy.

"Let me talk to my husband tonight, and can we get together soon and talk about the money?" Penny asked excitedly.

Now it was Mr. Glassman's turn to say what Penny usually said, "Sure." And as they were turning to go, he said, "Aren't you forgetting something? Some bread, some scones. On me, for the new owners of the bakery, if everything goes right."

Althea had to drive to the school, only a few blocks away. Penny was too excited. She was afraid she would drive up on the sidewalk or something, she was so nervous.

"Breathe, Honey," whispered Althea. "Breathe nice and slowly or you're gonna pass out! It will help you calm down." And she showed Penny how to breathe, nice and deep down into her belly, just like she had taught Tiffany and Reinaldo months before.

Buying the bakery was a big deal, they both knew, but if they wanted to keep making dozens of cookies every day, or more, maybe hundreds of cookies!, they needed to be able to make more at a time, or pretty soon they were going to be up until midnight every night, baking a dozen at a time in their kitchen stove.

Besides, where were they going to eat if the kitchen table and the counters were always covered with cookies? They needed their own cookie bakery!

That weekend, after Penny and Reinaldo and Tiffany spent all Saturday morning delivering cookies for parties and dinners and people who just wanted to eat them, Penny and Dan went for a meeting with Irving and Miriam Glassman. They met at the bakery, and sat down at a little table in the back, with mugs of coffee and blueberry muffins. ("These are good," thought Penny. "Maybe not magic, but really good. I wonder if they'll give their recipes?")

And they agreed on everything. The Glassmans were so excited to move on with their lives, and they already had a place picked out to move to. It meant a lot to them to sell their business to someone who loved baking and who would keep it as a bakery. So the price included mixers, big ones, and big ovens that could bake dozens of cookies at a time, big barrels of flour and sugar, and lists of all the places they bought those things.

"Oh dear," said the kindly Mrs. Glassman. "You can't buy your ingredients at the supermarket. That is much too expensive. You have to buy in bigger quantities, by the 100 pound barrel, not in one pound bags! You'll see, we'll stay a few weeks and help you while we pack our stuff and sell our house."

And just as Penny had stayed those extra weeks at the bank, helping the new person learn the job, the Glassmans stayed at the bakery, helping Penny, Althea and Nancy learn how to work all the machines, and how to place orders, and who delivers gas, and butter and fresh eggs, and all the other parts of running a bakery they didn't know.

Every day, instead of going home, Reinaldo and Tiffany walked to the bakery and helped finish the orders for the day.

And every night, they all went home together, tired from a full day's work but not really that hungry. Every one of them was snitching cookies!

Grand Opening

"We have to have a "grand Opening" said Tiffany one night at dinner. The Glassmans were going to leave in a few days, the bakery was officially going to be The Magic Cookie Factory, and a grand opening seemed like a great idea. They would have all the cookies and hot chocolate for the kids, and coffee for the grownups. They could get Asha Conroy to play her guitar and sing, they were sure of that since she lived in the neighborhood. And Althea added, "I would like to ask the monks to do a blessing, of the building, of the business, of the cookies and everyone who eats them." That seemed like a cool idea for a factory of magic cookies so they set a date for a Wednesday afternoon a week away. That would give them time to finish cleaning and decorating. There was still so much to do!

The open house would be from 3-6, so kids could come from school, and working people could come from work. They knew they had to have *plenty* of cookies that day.

For the next week, they lived at the Cookie Factory, just about. Nancy was there every day at nine, after leaving Miranda at school, and she, Penny and Althea painted the walls a soft buttery yellow, made beautiful purple curtains, painted stars on the walls, hung white Christmas lights and cleaned, cleaned, cleaned all the machines and glass showcases until the whole place shined like a jewel. And then it was time to bake!

Cookies, cookies and more cookies! There were all the regular ones, of course, the chocolate chips and oatmeal raisins, the peanut butter crunches and date bars, the apricot bars and double fudge brownies. There were lacy coconut macaroons and delicate shortbreads that melted in your mouth. Nancy brought her specialties, checkerboard cookies that came out like little teeny checkerboards of chocolate and vanilla dough. Tiffany found an old recipe for Mirror Cookies. Of course she liked the name, but they were kind of too much trouble, squeezing the jelly neatly into the hole in the center of the cookie, until she tasted them. Oh boy, were they good!

Reinaldo liked rolling dough and cutting out stars and moons of sugar cookies and crisp, chewy ginger cookies. Everyone found their favorite cookies to bake except Dan, who really didn't want to bake cookies at all. Every night after work he stopped at the Chinese restaurant, or the Mexican restaurant, or some restaurant and picked up dinner for the whole family, because they were still at the Factory, making cookies. Sometimes Nancy and Miranda were there, too. Miranda was only six, but she could still help stir.

"It's just for this week," Penny told Dan about the third night he brought dinner to the Factory.

"First it was my wife at the bank!" he growled. "Now it's my whole family! I'm going home to walk with Waffles, since I can't get any of you to come!"

"Group hug!" yelled Tiffany as she raced toward her father, flour all over her hands, her hair and her apron.

And then even Dan started laughing. "Where's an apron?" he asked. "One more person might make this go faster."

On Sunday, Althea and Reinaldo took a big bag of cookies, all the kinds they were making, to the monks and asked them if they could come to town on Wednesday afternoon and bless their new Magic Cookie Factory. Of course they were happy to do that, since they loved Althea, Reinaldo, Waffles and very much, the cookies. They said they would do a Tibetan blessing, and Reinaldo was really excited to see what that was. Althea offered to come pick them up with the truck, but the young monk told her no. "We will walk down," he said, "we are used to it. But you can drive us back, maybe with food bags because we do not have very much food left, and soon our visitors will come."

So they agreed, and Althea and Reinaldo went home.

"Where's the magic in all this?" you might ask. "How come they have to work so hard? Can't they make the broom do the baking, like in that movie with Mickey Mouse?"

But Althea didn't do magic like that, like making things do people's work, or making other people do people's work, either. Like I said, she *liked* baking cookies, she liked working hard, and most of all, she loved working with her whole family together. The magic was in the secret ingredient!

The day of the Grand Opening finally arrived. The monks walked down the mountain, as they promised, and brought a long trumpet looking horn and a drum. As three o'clock got near, they began to chant and play their instruments, then they walked around the building and said prayers at all the corners, by the back door and the big front door. They touched the windows, each one, and put their hands on the big front door while they chanted their prayers and waved incense in a metal bowl. All the kids who had walked there from school stood there spellbound. They had never seen the monks so close, in their robes, with their shaved heads, playing and chanting in a language they couldn't understand.

The doors opened and the monks went in first. Dozens of townspeople had gathered, young moms with babies in strollers and backpacks, old retired people out for a stroll and a free cookie, and all those kids. The monks took their time. They waved incense around the inside of the shop, blessing the air, adding a spicy exotic smell to the delicious one of cookies.

They walked into the bakery part and blessed each machine, the mixers, the ovens. They touched each one and said a prayer. They prayed the same thing as Althea, that everyone who ate these cookies would be happy and healthy. And they prayed for the success and happiness of their new friends with their new magic cookies.

When the chanting ended, and the drum stopped, all was quiet. Everyone felt the beautiful mysterious energy that had built up and stood silently. For a moment. Then a little girl tugged on her mother's hand and said in a loud voice, "Momma, I want a cookie!" and the spell was broken. Suddenly everyone wanted a cookie, or two, and a dozen to take home. The monks all had cookies, the kids had cookies, the moms and the retired people had cookies, and hot chocolate and coffee until it seemed there was nobody left in town who was not at the cookie factory.

Edgar left his restaurant to come. Irene, Ariel and Diane left the spa to the new receptionist, who was far too young and ditzy, according to Diane, even though they promised to bring her a cookie. Wally Brian's whole family came, his mom and dad and all five kids. That took some cookies! And you know all the people from the bank went straight from work to the cookie factory.

Cheryl Peterson hugged Penny with all her heart, even though she got flour on her work clothes. "I am so proud of you," she whispered. "You really give us all inspiration to go for it, and do what we love. Good for you!"

By the time 6 o'clock came, there wasn't a cookie or a brownie or a fruit bar left. The hot chocolate and coffee were all gone. There had been just the perfect amount. Everybody got exactly what they wanted, nobody the whole time was told "No, I'm sorry we're out of those." There was the perfect amount of cookies, and drinks and the perfect amount of people, too. It was magic!

Penny and the kids said they'd clean up, tired as they were, and then they were going out for dinner with Dan. They had to be at the cookie factory again first thing in the morning, because they were absolutely sold out of everything. The grand opening had been a total success.

Althea took the old truck to take the monks back home, as she agreed, because they needed to buy lots of food, and there was room in the back for all their stuff and they didn't mind riding in the back, anyway. It was a whole lot easier than walking. Penny and Althea had already decided to thank them for their blessing by buying their groceries this trip and sending them home with a whole bunch of cookies. They were so grateful.

They bought rice and tea and butter and flour, some meat and vegetables and bags of lentils. And chocolate. The oldest monk grinned at Althea sheepishly and held up a chocolate bar. "I like!" he told her, waving the bar around. Althea thought, "next time I go up there, I'll bring him chocolate from the cookie factory, some really good stuff!"

When they got out of the truck, each shouldering bags of rice and grocery bags of other stuff (the chocolate bar long gone!) there was a flurry of talk Althea couldn't understand. Then the young monk turned to her. "Please on Sunday in the afternoon bring your family and the dog, too, for eating Tibetan food with us. We like to feast with all your family. You can do?"

Althea nodded, very touched. Here they were, struggling to get by, and what pleased them was to share. "Yes," she told them. "We will come. Maybe even the girl who likes shopping best!" When the young monk translated for the others what she had said, they all laughed happily.

Then they turned, walking lightly in the darkness, each carrying a load, surefooted and strong. Althea watched them go and longed for the time she would be walking down that silent path with them, Instead, she turned the truck around and headed for a celebration dinner with the family at LuAnne's, a snazzy restaurant out on the lake that had food everyone in the family liked. They didn't do white tablecloths style dinners too often, since they were expensive, but tonight, they all deserved a celebration.

Sukoshi Rice

Winding Down

Sunday could not come soon enough for Althea. Even though she spent all day Thursday and Friday and half of Saturday baking up a storm, and making sure she had a good supply of cookies and chocolate bars to take for Sunday lunch with the monks, she just couldn't shake her nervous energy.

"This isn't like me," she thought as she squirmed on her meditation cushion in the mornings, unable to keep her eyes shut or her thoughts stilled for even a half a minute!

"This is definitely not like me," she thought when her hands started shaking when she was measuring flour and she shook it all over herself and the counter. "Maybe I have to stop drinking coffee."

By Saturday afternoon, when she had just finished burning a whole batch of coconut macaroons, she took off her apron, turned to Penny and said, "I'm getting out of here before I jinx the whole business. I don't know what is wrong with me, but if I am not better Monday, I might go see a doctor! I'm just a nervous wreck and you know me, I just don't *get* nervous!"

Penny and Tiffany watched her go, concern on their faces. Tiffany worked after school and on Saturdays, when they were only open until three, helping her mom with mixing and answering the phone. You might have thought she would hate it, getting flour and sugar on her clothes, but she didn't. She loved making cookies, too, and helping run a real business.

Just then a customer came in again, Michelle LeFevre, looking for two dozen cookies, for her Sunday dinner with her pastor and his family. Tiffany boxed them up for her, tying them with pretty bows, while Penny began turning off the ovens and mixers and closing up shop for the rest of the weekend.

They boxed up all the cookies that were left to take as a gift for lunch tomorrow. That had been the plan, and Althea had forgotten to do that, too. Penny was worried. She had never seen her mom so off center, nervous and shaky. She hoped it wasn't one of those horrible diseases they advertise on TV! She had to smile at that thought. Althea was the healthiest woman she knew. Not just for her age, for any age. It was probably nothing major. It would probably pass.

For her part, Althea had forgotten she rode to the factory with Penny and Tiffany. Since she didn't have a car there, not even the old truck, which Dan and Reinaldo were using for hauling some furniture for their friends the Washingtons from up the street, she started walking. She walked and walked and walked and walked and all of a sudden noticed she had been holding her breath for the last couple of days. She took a huge deep breath and started to feel better. Another one, and she didn't feel crazy anymore at all. Another one, and her walking slowed and she felt calm again, just like her own self.

Just then a car slowed down next to her. "Hey Grandma," yelled Tiffany, "C'mon, get in! I'll move over."

So she did, and she told Penny and Tiffany she felt much better, that she had just forgotten her own advice and walking and breathing put her right back on track. But in the back of her mind, she had to wonder why she had forgotten to breathe. She never did that any more. Was the planet tilting? Were the stars shifting in the sky? What was the energy shift that had knocked her so off center she spilled flour, burned cookies, got careless and shaky and forgot to breathe?

When they got home, Althea announced she was taking a long hot bath, then doing some stretching and meditating. She looked at Penny, "We've been too busy to start you meditating, not that I am any great advertisement for it today! But I am happy to teach you what I know when you want."

"Thanks, Mom," Penny smiled back, "right now I think a nap is more in order. We sure have had a busy week."

Althea got in the tubful of hot water and felt her muscles unknotting from all the hours of standing and mixing and baking (and burning, which takes energy, too!!) She closed her eyes, feeling quiet and still, when she noticed the water starting to make little waves and eddies. "Now this is plain odd!" she thought. As she opened her eyes, she watched waves getting bigger and bigger, threatening to splash over the sides, threatening to go right over her. She lay there still, then whispered, "Tenzin."

Immediately, the waves stopped. The water got still. All was quiet. Tenzin was near. DUH!!! He knocked flour out of her hands, burned cookies and almost swamped her in her own bath before she got the message. She wasn't crazy, she just wasn't paying attention. Her magic was a little rusty, but she was looking forward to getting it back up to speed. Now she was excited, but not nervous. Now that she knew there was a reason for all the shaking, she was so happy to go find that reason, wherever he was.

Sunday at the Monastery

Everyone was happy the day was so clear, even if it still was a little cold. It was noon before they started for the monastery, since everyone had a busy morning. Penny and Tiffany had gone to church, which they loved to do. Dan and Reinaldo had offered to finish the moving job for the Washingtons, so they took off early to get that done. And Althea had meditated for a long time, then dressed in Tibetan and Nepalese clothes that had been pretty much hanging in her closet since she got back. It was easier to go to town in sweatpants or jeans and a sweater or t-shirt than to wear robes and have everyone stare, even though it was a polite and friendly town!

Since it was chilly, and it would be even colder up the mountain, Tiffany dressed in so many layers of fluff and fuzz she looked like a very cute poodle. Dan and Penny had on parkas and gloves, carried bottles of water and a cell phone. The family had already had enough accidents on Overlook Mountain, what with Dan's heart and Althea's ankle. They weren't taking any chances. Reinaldo was dancing around with impatience, trying to get everyone moving, which made Waffles dance around and bark. Finally, they were all in the car.

The monks had made sure the path was clear. Althea could see where they had brushed the last bits of snow from the rocks, so they would be safe. She was very grateful, even though the rest of the family didn't seem to notice.

As they came into the clearing of the monastery, they could see the monks behind the building where they had built a fire. The delicious smell of roasting meat and vegetables came to them, and Waffles ran ahead, hoping something had fallen. The men all looked up and waved, and then from behind them, one stepped forward.

He looked up the path at them and then shouted, "ALLEE!!!!!" and began to run toward Althea. She shoved her box of cookies at Tiffany and began to run down the path, shouting "Tenzin!!!" The monks, Dan and Penny stood there with their mouths open! What was going on?

You see, even with all those months living together, Althea had never told Dan and Penny she had a man in her life. Tiffany knew, and still rolled her eyes about it, and of course Reinaldo knew because they had met, even if it was in dreams, but Penny and Dan had no idea. So there was Althea, hugging the daylights out of a Tibetan guy, both of them in robes and boots, and Penny thought she might just faint!

But as they came down to the clearing, Althea took Tenzin's hand and said, "This is my friend from Nepal, Tenzin. Well, more than friend, but...." and she introduced him to Dan, whose hand he shook and said, "Bury nice to meet you," and to Penny, to whom he bowed and said, "Bury nice to meet you," and to Tiffany, to whom he bowed and said, "Oh so beauty Tiffany" which made her blush and like him very much, and to Reinaldo, who got a big hug. They looked each other in the eyes, and the young eyes and the old eyes crinkled up with delight. "Ahh, Reinaldo!" exclaimed Tenzin. "Ahh Tenzin!" said Reinaldo. And not to be left out, Waffles came running up. Tenzin turned and patted him, calling him something that sounded like Waffou.

Then he turned to the monks, all standing there wondering what in the world was going on with the new guy, who had just arrived to help them and already seemed to have a girlfriend! He said something that sounded like woo woo onna gee gee wonko, but what he really said was, "Hey guys, this is my beloved lady from Nepal I was telling you about."

The monks were delighted. They already loved Althea and the whole family so to find out she was the mystery woman was the frosting on the cake.

They had roasted a lamb, which normally Althea wouldn't eat when she had a choice, but she knew how much trouble they had gone to preparing this feast. And besides, it smelled delicious. She and Tenzin held hands and sat so close together they looked like someone had glued their robes at the seams. The food was delicious, lamb and vegetables and flat bread baked right on the fire, lots of hot buttered tea and of course, cookies. Tenzin could speak much better English than she remembered, and when she told him so, he said, "I practice. For you."

Reinaldo sat on his other side, and kept sneaking peeks at Tenzin's face. He was handsome in a laughing, crinkly kind of way. Once, when Reinaldo peeked, Tenzin was waiting for him, popping his eyes at him in the funniest way that got them both laughing like crazy.

They were all sitting in a circle near the fire, Penny and Dan and Tiffany in the old lawn chairs Althea had brought months before, everyone else on logs or on mats on the ground. The young monk who spoke good English sat next to Penny and Dan, explaining who everyone was, and where they came from, and how they got to this little monastery on top of the mountain in their little town. Tiffany was wandering around, or sat with them and listened, politely, although the man had an accent she found a little hard to understand! The rest of the monks, and the two newcomers were chatting away when all of a sudden Tenzin tapped his spoon on his mug to get everyone's attention.

When everyone was quiet, he said, "wazoo monta zeelo" or something like that, which meant,

"My family." He waved his arm to include all the Tibetans.

"My famaree," he said in English that was a little fuzzy, but not bad, waving his arm again to include Dan, Penny, Tiffany and Reinaldo.

Then he kneeled in front of Althea and reached in his pocket. Out he pulled the most amazing ring. It was made of color and light and sent out shining bright sparkles. "Allee," he said, his name for her since Althea was just too complicated. "Please will marry me?"

Althea threw her arms around him and said, "Yes!" with such great enthusiasm she knocked him over, and everyone laughed and hugged with the good news. Only Reinaldo looked a little worried, until Tenzin and Althea noticed and reached over to pull him into their big hug.

While the monks cleaned up, and the young one showed Dan and Penny and Tiffany the inside of their little monastery, Tenzin, Althea and Reinaldo, with Waffles along, walked up to the little ridge that looked down on the main building. "House here," said Tenzin clearly. "Door here, look to mountains." Reinaldo could just see it! "No more snow, make house."

Sukoshi Rice

Springtime

When it finally looked like it might stay thawed for a while, it was time to start a house, a little house, for Tenzin and Althea. Dan and Reinaldo came up in the truck, looking for the closest they could get to the monastery. They didn't know how in the world (magic?) the monks had managed to build their place with no road nearby. Did they carry everything on their backs for a mile and a half of trails? There had to be an easier way.

That afternoon, they found it. There was a trail below the monastery that came pretty close. They only drove down about half a mile, but Dan figured a couple of men with chainsaws, machetes or handsaws, and they would have a road they could use in just a few days work. Building a house was going to be fun!

And it wasn't just the house. The monastery needed more room. It had been crowded with 4, but now, with 7, it was packed. Sometimes Tenzin stayed at the house with them, where he really enjoyed the TV most of all. He liked travel programs and animal programs, and even cooking programs. Just like Althea, he did not like the news. He would listen, not understanding it all, but some, then turn to whoever was there, usually Reinaldo who went anywhere Tenzin went, and say, "Not true. Talking not true." Reinaldo would say, "We say, that is a lie, Tenzin." "Yes," he nodded, "Man talking a lie."

` And he liked cartoons, very much. He had seen TV of course, but this was so clear, and so big! Having a big TV in the living room, and smaller ones around the house, and computers too made him realize it was true what he had heard about America, that the people were all very rich. They all had cars, and closets full of clothes, and furniture so soft you just went to sleep sitting in a chair. There were so many things he didn't understand the need for, like machines to wash the dishes and machines to wash the clothes, but in a very short while, he liked them just fine!

Althea went with him to the store to buy some clothes that might help with people staring when they saw them together. They might stare anyway, with his brown crinkly face and laughing eyes, and at her wild hair and big smile, but at least if they dressed like other people they wouldn't stand out quite so much! And besides, nothing beats jeans and work boots when you are clearing a road and building a house.

There were other people in town who had become friends with the Tibetans, and they started showing up that spring to help. Dan actually got Wally Brian's father Al to ride up and cut some brush. He was pretty glad to get out of a Saturday at home with five kids in the house and besides, like most people, he was curious. What were the Tibetans like? How did they live up there on that cold mountainside, and why? What did they eat? What did they believe? People really wondered.

Most people wondered in a really friendly curious way, 'cause that's what most people are like. But some people didn't bother wondering or finding anything out. Some people decided anyone different from them was bad and had to be driven away, or at least picked on and bullied.

There were three big stupid boys in the high school named Duane, Jesse and Billy. They really weren't nice. Billy wasn't really mean, but he wanted Duane and Jesse to like him so he acted like them. Tiffany and her friends called them Dumb, Dumber and Dumbest, which also wasn't very nice, but so far, they deserved it. Those boys were always ganging up on smaller kids, pushing them around, and just being bullies.

One afternoon, Penny left Althea and Tenzin at the store. She was going to pick up Reinaldo at school, then deliver a huge cookie order to the bank so she could say hi to all her old pals. Tiffany was going to Becca's to do homework. Everybody knew that meant more clothes, boys and makeup talk than homework, but as long as her grades stayed good that was ok.

After Penny drove away, Tenzin loaded the last cookie trays of the day into the ovens and told Althea he'd be right back. They were out of coffee and he was just going to run across the street to the neighborhood market and get enough for the rest of the afternoon. Of course, it was cheaper to wait until the delivery truck came the next morning, but he really wanted a cup of coffee. With a cookie.

As he walked out of the bakery, he saw three very large, overgrown boys leaning against an old pickup truck, watching the store and watching him. They were waiting for him. They'd seen him in the bakery and they were just itching to start a fight. He was a small man. They figured he'd be easy to push around, just for a little fun, something to do after school.

"Hey Chinaman," Jesse called out, pulling his eyes out to the sides to make them look slanted, like Tenzin's.

"Ohhh, not Chinese," replied Tenzin with a friendly smile.

"Ohhh, not Chinese," mocked Duane, towering over Tenzin with his big belly hanging out. "Well whatever you are, you don't belong here! This is our town!"

Blocking his path, the three big boys surrounded Tenzin, who was much shorter and lighter than any of them. All he wanted to do was go to the grocery store and get some coffee, but there were these three hulking obstacles in his path.

"Ah, please excuse me, boys," said Tenzin politely, but they crowded in on him even more, their bodies inches from his, their faces looming over him, full of meanness. Penny drove up just then to drop Reinaldo off, since he told her he'd much rather be at the bakery with Tenzin and his grandma than go to the bank. Penny and Reinaldo saw Tenzin surrounded by three large, menacing boys. Penny yelled, "Hey, leave him alone!"

From inside the store, Althea heard Penny yell. She came to the door, pretty much covered in flour and going wild, she started yelling right away. "What is going on here? You boys go away!"

Before he could remember to shut his own mouth, Jesse yelled back, "Shut up old lady, this doesn't concern you!"

BAM! Jesse flew backward and crashed into the side of the pickup truck, but nobody had touched him! Duane leaned over into Tenzin's face, "You stinking little Chinaman, look what you did!"

BAM! Duane hit the side of the pickup truck and slid down to sit next to his pal Jesse on the sidewalk.

Billy backed up a few steps and put his hands up. "I'm good! I'm good!" He couldn't believe what he'd just seen. The little man had barely moved. He hadn't touched his two big friends at all, and they had flown through the air and were collapsed against the truck.

"Ok man, I'm really sorry. I'm sorry we were so rude." Turning to Althea, who had a funny look on her face, he stammered, "I'm sorry M'am, I'm sorry my friend was so rude." Althea just looked at him then turned back to look at Tenzin, like he was someone she thought she knew, but didn't. Reinaldo and Penny were giving him the same look. Who was this guy they thought they knew?

Billy couldn't help himself. Turning back to Tenzin he asked, "What did you just do? What was that called? Can you teach me to do it?"

Tenzin bowed slightly to Billy, smiled and answered "Not for bad people to know." Billy just stood there with his mouth kind of hanging open. The last thing he wanted in that moment was to be bad, or to ever be bad again, even if it meant Jesse and Duane didn't like him anymore. Who cares about them? He just wanted to be good so he could be like that little man they thought they could bully and push around. Boy, had he surprised them!

Reinaldo stared. He had seen Tenzin collect energy in waves, then send it out to move those boys. Or maybe Tenzin didn't really collect it. It collected around him, like iron filings drawn to a magnet. The waves of energy moved through the air like jello, smacking into Jesse and Duane, lifting them into the air and slamming them against the truck. Tenzin didn't have to touch them. It was something Reinaldo had heard about, like "The Force," but he had just seen it with his own eyes. He was just about to ask his mom, "Did you see that?" when Tenzin caught his eye. With a teeny tilt of his head, he let Reinaldo know not to say anything yet.

By the time Jesse and Duane came to their senses and were standing up again, Billy was halfway home, running. He didn't want to be friends with them anymore. That little man had told him he wouldn't teach this thing to bad people, and

Billy decided then and there to only do good things. No more fighting, only helping. Maybe then he'd get to learn what that man knew about how to win a fight without even having to touch someone. And besides, he wanted to be like that guy, smiling the whole time, so polite and kind as he sent bad guys sailing through the air. Billy wanted to be that kind of guy, not the big kind who picked on little guys and bullied people. He was done with that! He didn't know how in the world he'd ever convince that little man to teach him, but for the moment, he knew enough to put some distance between himself and the boys he thought were his friends only minutes before.

Tenzin waited for Duane and Jesse to get up. Both boys eyed him warily. Were they going to be sent through the air again? How had that guy done that? They didn't know what to say. Nobody had ever taught them to say "I'm sorry" when they did something bad. They always thought they could say what they wanted and do what they wanted because they were bigger than the people they picked on. Well, they'd just picked on a little guy, pretty old, too, and he'd sent them flying. They had a lot to think about.

Tenzin, Althea and Penny stood silently, looking at them. Finally Duane said, "We're sorry. We were rude but we won't do it again."

Tenzin nodded then, and they knew they could leave. After they hurried to their truck and drove away, without looking back, Althea turned to Tenzin. "What was that?" she wanted to know.

"Boys rude to you. Needed lesson."

"Yes," she smiled at him. "Thank you for defending me. You know the word defending? Yes? Good. But what was that you did to them? How did you make them fly through the air without touching them? What was that called?"

Tenzin smiled back, crinkling his eyes at her. "That called teaching a lesson."

Then he smiled again. "Now, I go for coffee. Come, Reinaldo, we go to coffee store."

As they left, Penny was getting back in her car to get those cookies to the bank, and Althea was going in to the bakery to take out the last cookies of the day so they could clean up and go home.

Tenzin smiled at Reinaldo. "You saw," was all he said. Reinaldo nodded his head, wide eyed. "Someday I teach. You and good bad boy. You want?"

The look of happiness in Reinaldo's eyes was enough answer. Someday he would know how to move energy like that. It was the most exciting thing he could imagine. He could hardly wait to start.

Photo courtesy of Ebru Yildiz

About the Author:

Sukoshi Rice lives in a small mountain town in Western North Carolina with her faithful sidekick, Mimi, thinking up stories.

Made in the USA
Columbia, SC
27 July 2019